Praise for **Christina Kilbourne's**
Dear Jo: The story of losing Leah ... and searching for hope.

"... rings authentic and true ... an important book that every teen, young adult and parent should read." – *Windsor Life*

"It is powerful without being preachy." – *Children's Literature*

"... a terrific, readable plot and is also able to deal sensitively with a current and serious social problem ... combines mystery, adventure and high emotion while educating readers at the same time."
– *CM: Canadian Review of Materials*

"... a strong message but it doesn't interfere with the storytelling ... compelling." – *School Library Journal*

"... an all too real account of the dangers that lurk inside Internet chat rooms ..." – *The Globe and Mail*

"Kilbourne tenderly explores a difficult subject in a novel that culminates in healing." – *Montreal Review of Books*

Selected, Ontario Library Association's "Best Bets for 2007"

Shortlisted, Manitoba Young Readers' Choice Awards

Winner, Best Novel, "Get the Lead Out" Literary Awards

Selected, Resource Links: The Year's Best

Dear Jo: *The story of losing Leah ... and searching for hope.*

1-897073-51-3

ilable now.

THEY CALLED ME RED

They Called Me Red
Text © 2008 Christina Kilbourne

Published by Lobster Press™
1620 Sherbrooke Street West, Suites C & D
Montréal, Québec   H3H 1C9
Tel. (514) 904-1100 • Fax (514) 904-1101 • www.lobsterpress.com

Publisher: Alison Fripp
Editor: Meghan Nolan
Editorial Assistants: Emma Stephen and Brynn Smith-Raska
Graphic Design & Production: Tammy Desnoyers

We acknowledge the financial support of the Government of Canada through the Book Publishing Industry Development Program (BPIDP) for our publishing activities.

We acknowledge the support of the Canada Council for the Arts for our publishing program.

The Canada Council | Le Conseil des Arts
for the Arts | du Canada

Library and Archives Canada Cataloguing in Publication

Kilbourne, Christina, 1967-
   They called me Red / Christina Kilbourne.

ISBN 978-1-897073-88-9

   I. Title.
PS8571.I476T44 2008   jC813'.6   C2008-901096-5

Printed and bound in Canada.

Text is printed on Rolland Enviro 100 Book, 100% recycled post-consumer fibre.

To the redheads in my life: Dave, Greg, Josh, Callie, and, especially, Leo

– Christina Kilbourne

THEY CALLED ME RED

written by
Christina Kilbourne

Lobster Press™

Each year, more than two million children are exploited in the global commercial sex trade.

Trafficking in Persons Report
United States of America, Department of State
June 2007

According to sources from UNICEF and Vietnam's Ministry of Justice as well as other groups, as many as 400,000 Vietnamese women and children have been trafficked overseas, most since the end of the Cold War. They are smuggled to Cambodia, China, Hong Kong, Macau, Malaysia, Taiwan, the Czech Republic – and, to a lesser extent, the United States – for commercial sexual exploitation.

Andrew Lam
Pacific News Service
July 19, 2005

Red is the what they called the color of my hair,
even though it's really orange.
Red is what they called me. They didn't use my name.
They just called me Red.
I was the house specialty because of my red hair,
because of my white skin.
But it was my red hair that helped me in the end.
This is my story.

Before My Story Started

Life was pretty good until Lily came along. We didn't have much spending money and I had to do a lot of stuff around the apartment because Dad worked so much, but we were pretty happy. Lily ruined that. She took over a little at a time until nothing could be the same ever again.

I grew up with just my dad. It had always been him and me since I could remember. My mom disappeared when I was still a baby. Dad said she was a drug addict – the worst kind who traded anything for a hit – so he said it was best she'd left. At least that's what he told me when I asked about her. He said he worried about me when he was at work during the days, worried she'd trade me for a bag of crack. So when he came home one day and found me crying in my crib in an empty apartment, he picked me up and promised me a better life. He left a note and left the scene. I guess technically *we* ran away, but he said even when he tried to track her down in the following months, it was as if she'd melted into a puddle on the street, and he figured she was dead. He even *told* me she was dead one day. I was in Kindergarten when I finally realized that all the other kids had moms. I tried to ask questions back then, to find out more about her, but Dad never wanted to talk and I just gave up wanting to know.

When I was a kid, Dad worked at a slaughter house on the edge of the city. He was big and tall and that helped him get a job quartering the animal carcasses. It wasn't glamorous or anything, but, like he said, it "paid the rent and put food on the table and clothes on our backs." It even bought me a new skateboard once. People might think that a man his size who cut up dead animals all day would be mean and rough, but he wasn't. I don't remember him yelling at me once when I was little, not even when I had one of my temper tantrums. Instead, whenever he got mad, he'd pause, take a deep breath, then lower his voice. I'd have to shut up just so I could hear him.

All of my friends loved my dad – Cody, Eric, and Vic especially. When I got a little older Dad was happy when they came over to hang out at our place. He even let us have a big party every May to celebrate all of our birthdays at once. He was the kind of guy who put food out for stray dogs and let the neighbor's cat come into our apartment, even though half its tail was missing.

Once, when I was eight, I had to make a papier-mâché fish for a school project. I'd chosen a porcupine fish and was having trouble keeping the toothpicks in place while I laid the first strips of wet newspaper over the balloon. I'd started to cry and was ready to give up when Dad came to help. It took us two hours and by then the entire kitchen was covered in flour. But we finished and the teacher was so impressed, she put it in the trophy case by the front doors. I stopped to look at it every day on my way home.

Dad had such a big heart that he'd help anyone who needed it like that.

It was that same heart that got us into trouble.

Part 1: Lily

CHAPTER 1

Dad met Lily at the meat works, which was what he called his job when he talked to people like teachers and neighbors. She worked in the office taking orders for the quartered carcasses. To look at Lily, with her perfectly brushed hair and painted fingernails, you'd think she'd hate to work in such a place. But that would mean you didn't really know her.

Lily was the first lady who ever worked at the slaughterhouse. Usually, the owner managed the office. But then he had a heart attack and his wife hired a temp. They sent Lily. She was only supposed to be there a few weeks, but then business starting coming in from unexpected places and they extended her contract. Dad started spending his coffee breaks with her, then his lunches. He'd never really met someone from a faraway country before. Her real name was *Hue* but she changed it to Lily when she came to the United States. She said *Hue* meant Lily in Vietnamese but that "Lily" sounded prettier. Dad was impressed that she had another name and could speak another language, that she ate dumplings with sticks and drank tea that smelled like flowers. Once he met her, she was all he could talk about. He started to sound like an advertisement for her.

I wasn't used to him talking about women, and he'd never had a girlfriend before, so his obsession with Lily freaked me out. When he told me he'd like to invite her over for dinner one night, I complained that he'd gone girl crazy. But he smiled and said we needed a woman's touch in our lives, that I could use a mother.

"But I don't even want a mother," I protested.

"That's because you don't know any different."

"What's so great about a mother anyway?" I asked.

"They make a place home. They make a family real."

"I like it being just you and me. You're like a mom *and* a dad."

"Moms just understand kids better. They think of things that Dads don't."

"But you think of everything already. I'm like the luckiest kid I know."

"Can you trust me this one time? Give Lily a chance?"

"Okay," I said reluctantly and then we hugged hard like we might never let go of each other. I gave up arguing because I knew I wasn't going to convince him that things were great the way they were – that a single guy and a ten-year-old boy were better off on their own.

The Saturday Lily was set to come over was a complete write-off. Dad spent the entire day fussing over everything: how clean the dishes were, how dirty the walls were, how worn our furniture was.

"It's how we live," I said. "If she doesn't like it, that's her problem."

"But I want to make a good impression."

"Why?"

"Because I want her to be impressed."

"Why?"

"I dunno. Because I care about what she thinks. Because I care about her."

"But you hardly know her."

"That's the point. If I can impress her a little, then maybe I can get to know her. Then maybe she'll be impressed for real."

He looked so nervous that I decided to suck it up and not say anything else. I didn't even tease him when he put on his apron and started cooking. Normally I couldn't resist, but he always said the same thing: it was better than ruining another pair of pants.

When Lily came in the apartment that evening, she stared at me. She didn't even try to hide her curiosity about my hair, and every time I got close, she reached out to touch it.

"Such a beautiful color red," she said in her strange accent.

"If you look close, you can see it's really orange," I tried to say politely.

More than anything, I hated to be called a redhead.

"No, silly. It's red. It sparkles like fire," she said.

I cringed and Dad laughed.

I could tell he was trying to make us like each other.

"Whatever you call it, women in my country would pay an arm and a leg for it," she said.

"They can have it," I told her.

"And what do you call the color of your eyes?" she asked and stared into them the way the doctor did the time I had pink eye and I ended up having to get eye drops.

"I dunno. Blue?" I said and pulled back.

"I think they're more gray," she said, moving in close again.

"Whatever. I never really looked that close." I turned away.

"Gray like a storm cloud," she announced triumphantly. "Very unusual."

"That's my kid," Dad said as he chuckled. "Stormy and fiery." Then he served up plates of his homemade ravioli and tomato sauce.

I hated that Dad sided with her. I wanted to run to my room and slam my door, but somehow I found a way to keep sitting, though I didn't dare look up at her again in case she started talking about my freckles next.

Dad tried his best to find something we could all talk about, but Lily was clueless. She didn't know a thing about any sports – not baseball, basketball, or football. She didn't know about skateboarding, video games, or hip hop. She'd never even heard of Tony Hawk. All she did that night was pick at her food and say she'd do the cooking next time.

Lily was short and thin and she looked young too. She had smooth skin, black hair and she giggled like a teenager whenever Dad spoke. Dad thought it was cute, but I thought it was annoying. Sitting with them at the table was like being trapped in one of those bad romantic comedies Vic's mother loved to watch, only I wasn't laughing and nobody noticed.

When dinner was over, Dad walked her to the bus stop. He wasn't gone long, and I hoped it would be their last date. But when he came back, he had a foolish look on his face. I gagged on the lump that rose in my throat. I had a bad feeling about Lily.

CHAPTER 2

The next day, Dad woke me up early and said he wanted to go to the library. He hadn't been to the library since I was probably in about Grade Two, so of course I was suspicious.

"Why do you want to go to the library on a Sunday morning? And why at nine o'clock?"

"I dunno. To use the computers ... do some reading."

"Is it even open this early?"

"It opens at ten. I thought we could stop for breakfast on the way."

"You want *me* to come?"

"Of course I want you to come. We always spend our Sundays together."

"Yeah, but not at the library," I protested.

I mean, sure we made a point of spending every Sunday afternoon doing some dad-and-son thing, like going to the computer store at the mall to try out their new video games, watching old movies, or batting balls at the park. But I didn't think the library would count – especially not so early.

"You must have some homework you can do," he persisted. "C'mon, get up. When we're done we can see what's playing at the movies."

I dragged myself out of bed and we walked down the busy sidewalk in silence. It was late May, so the market on the corner had tables of fruit outside and we had to wait to get past the people shopping. When we walked through the door of the diner, Dad bumped me playfully on the shoulder. I smiled up at him, though I wasn't through being suspicious.

"What's it going to be: pancakes or the special?" he asked me.

"The special."

"Bacon or sausage?"

"Sausage."

"That's my boy," he said and we sat down at a table in the front window where we could watch the traffic pass by.

"Maybe we can get a couple of custard-filled donuts to go," Dad suggested while we waited for our breakfasts to arrive.

I looked at the donuts behind the counter and nodded. More than any other donut, those were our favorites.

Dad smiled all the way through his coffee until I didn't think I could stand it a second longer. I studied his face close, trying to see him the way a stranger might see him, the way Lily saw him. He had light blue eyes and thick black hair cut close to his head. His chin was almost always covered in a day's worth of stubble because he hated to shave, and he had a t-shaped scar over his left eyebrow from a bike accident when he was young.

"Does this trip to the library have anything to do with Lily?" I finally asked.

"Well, yes, actually. She invited us over for an 'authentic' Vietnamese meal next weekend and I thought it would be good to read up on Vietnam, find out what else it's known for besides a war, and figure out what we might be eating."

I rolled my eyes and dipped toast into my egg yolk. "One dinner and she's got you turning into a computer geek," I said.

"I'm not turning into anything. I just think it would be nice if we knew a little bit about where she comes from. Look, she knows all about our country"– he gave a sweep of his arm as if the diner was our country –"we should make an effort to know something about hers."

"I thought you said I could do my schoolwork?" I said, trying to find a way out of having to read up on Vietnam.

"I did. But I noticed you didn't bring any."

"I could still do some research. I've got an English project coming up."

"Okay, then. I'll tell you what I learn."

I rolled my eyes again and finished eating. Dad ignored me. He wasn't going to let anything ruin his good mood.

After breakfast we walked to the library in silence. He nodded at the people who passed us on the sidewalk, and the uneasy feeling in my stomach returned: I'd never seen him so happy before.

The librarian was just unlocking the doors when we arrived, so the building was empty and all the computers were free. I sat at a computer in the corner and Dad picked the one next to me. I angled my screen away and logged onto the Tony Hawk web site to see if there were any more entries in his road journal. Dad leaned over after a few minutes.

"You have to do a school project on skateboarding?" he asked.

"Uh, yeah. We have to write a report on the sport of our choice."

"Right," he said.

For a slaughterhouse guy without a computer, Dad was pretty good at surfing the Internet. Within minutes he was spouting facts about Vietnam. He told me stuff about the traffic problems, especially in the big cities; stuff about average incomes; stuff about how much it rained, which was a lot; he even told me what the main entrees were, and they all sounded to me as if they all consisted of rice.

"Keep your voice down or you're gonna get us kicked out," I complained finally.

"Relax," he said and smiled at the librarian.

"Devon?"

I looked up and was surprised to see Vic standing behind us.

"What are *you* doing here?" I asked him.

He blushed and nodded toward the stacks of movies behind us.

"Mom's getting another dumb romance movie. Dad's taking us to a hockey game tonight and she doesn't want to come."

"Bummer you got dragged along," I said as I eyed Dad.

"Yeah, I guess. What are you guys doing?" he asked.

Dad turned in his chair. "We're doing *research*," he said as if he was making an announcement to the entire library.

"Why?"

"To expand our minds," he said with a bit of sarcasm.

Vic smiled. "Tony Hawk is expanding Devon's mind?"

"*I'm* expanding my mind. Devon's working on his English project," Dad said and looked at me.

"What project?" Vic asked.

"He has to write a report on the sport of his choice. Aren't you in his English class?"

Vic glanced at me and I hung my head. I knew I was busted.

"Oh, yeah. I did mine already. I forgot."

"Nice try," Dad said and turned back to the computer.

Vic and I locked eyes.

"Sorry," he mouthed. Then out loud he said, "Well, I gotta go. Mom's got two days worth of movies already. See ya later."

"See ya," I said.

"Hope you get an A on that report," Dad called after him.

I slumped in my seat. I knew Dad wasn't really mad at me, and that I wouldn't catch crap or anything, but I hated to get caught lying just the same.

"Can we go now?" I asked after a few more minutes.

"Soon. I just want to look up Ho Chi Minh City," Dad said before he got hooked again on the computer screen. "That's where Lily's from. Maybe if we know something about where she used to live, we'll have more to talk about next weekend."

I sighed and knew our chance of going to the movies was slipping away.

CHAPTER 3

The following Saturday we arrived at Lily's place at five o'clock. She lived in a one-bedroom apartment in an old house. Her apartment was at the back and had low ceilings, which wasn't a problem for Lily or me, but Dad had to duck his head when he stepped inside.

Whatever Lily was cooking smelled good, and even though I wanted her dinner to be a disaster, my stomach growled. I couldn't wait to eat. While I looked around, she worked in the kitchen, and Dad asked over and over if there was something he could do to help.

"You sit. You cooked last week. I cook this week," she said.

I thought she sounded bossy, but Dad beamed.

I picked up a photograph of two boys sitting on a bed.

"Who are these kids?" I asked.

"My boys, Quan and Sang. They're twelve now, like you," Lily said as she came and took the photo from me.

I didn't bother to correct her, to tell her I had only *just* turned eleven. Adults never understand the difference one year makes.

"You have kids?" I asked and looked around.

"Yes. Still in Vietnam. I'm saving to bring them here soon."

"Who's taking care of them?"

"My parents."

"When did you see them last?"

"Two years ago. Then I came here."

"You haven't seen your kids in two years?"

"I'm making a better life. It's worth the sacrifice. Now sit and stop asking so many questions."

I looked to see if Dad noticed the way she spoke to me, but he hadn't. I wondered if I was being too sensitive. I didn't have long to dwell on it, though, because she appeared with gigantic bowls of steaming soup and set them down on the table in front of Dad and me.

"What is it?" I asked as I stared into my bowl.

"Vietnamese rare beef soup."

"It's raw meat?"

"Not raw. Rare. The heat of the soup will cook it. Wait and see."

Dad picked up his spoon and started to eat.

"What else is in it?" I asked.

"Pork dumplings, rice noodles, basil leaves, and bean sprouts," Lily said between mouthfuls.

"It's delicious," Dad said as he wiped sweat from his forehead.

I took a small sip. It tasted safe, so I scooped up a bigger mouthful. Soon I was slurping back rice noodles and sipping tea the way she and Dad were.

When we finished eating, Dad helped Lily with the dishes. I stayed at the table, trying not to look bored and wondering how long I'd have to listen to them talk, when Dad said we should be leaving.

"It's a thirty-minute bus ride home and Devon gets pretty crabby if he doesn't get enough sleep," he teased.

I was annoyed at him for saying such a thing, but I smiled and played along, relieved that the night was over.

On the bus I kept thinking about Lily leaving her kids in Vietnam. I couldn't imagine being away from Dad for a couple of weeks, never mind a couple of years.

"Did you know she had kids?" I asked, after a few blocks. "I mean, did she ever mention them to you before?"

I was sitting next to the window watching my reflection against the darkness and beyond that, the store fronts passing by. Dad was sitting beside me.

"Yeah, last week. We hadn't decided what to tell you though."

"What do you mean *you hadn't decided what to tell me*?"

"Lily didn't want to tell you about them until you got to know her a little better. She's afraid you'll think she's a terrible mother for leaving them behind. But I didn't want to hide anything from you, so we were going to tell you tonight. Then you saw that picture."

"Yeah, right," I said.

"It's the truth, Devon. Lily's really concerned you don't like her. I told her you'd just take some time to get used to her."

"She's not easy to get used to. She's sort of ... well ... mean when she talks to me, and she makes funny noises in her throat, like, when she's thinking."

"She doesn't intend to be mean and she doesn't *make* funny noises. It's just her way. Besides, I don't think she's used to kids speaking their minds like you do. But I want you to understand she didn't leave her boys because she wanted to. She left because she thought they could do better over here in the long run. She misses them a lot. It's not easy on her."

"What are they like?"

"She hasn't really said that much. She said they were going to school and living with her parents. They work too, so they can help pay their way. She mostly talks about how much she misses them."

"You don't think it's strange that she left them behind like that? That she hasn't seen them in over two years?"

"Look, I don't think I can understand what life was like for her as a single mom in Vietnam, so I try not to judge. She made the best decision she could at the time."

"What happened to their father?"

"He took off or something. I don't know exactly. She doesn't like to talk about it and sometimes it's better not to ask too many questions. I didn't exactly tell her about our past either, you know."

CHAPTER 4

From that point on, Lily was a regular part of our lives – a little bit at first, then more and more until she was at our apartment every day and spent most nights, too. On one of those nights, when we were watching a Christmas special on TV, Dad told Lily she was wasting money renting a place that was empty all the time.

"If you moved in here you'd be able to save faster and bring Quan and Sang over sooner," he blurted out.

Lily's face lit up like a Christmas tree and she cuddled closer to him on the couch.

"I'd like that. I'm always so lonely when I go home at night."

He put his arm around her shoulder and they kissed. I hated to see them touch, so I looked away, then waited a moment before sneaking off to my bedroom. I closed my door gently and looked up at the ceiling. Tears burned in my eyes and I tried hard not to cry.

"Devon?" Dad knocked, then came in.

I turned away.

"Listen, I'm sorry. I didn't plan to say that. It just sort of came out."

I kept my back to him and sat down at my desk. I opened the drawer and fiddled with a bunch of pens.

"It doesn't have to be forever. Just until she has enough money to bring the boys over, and then we can see from there."

I knew he was watching me, so I nodded. He waited a moment and when I didn't speak, he left. I heard the door close and when I knew I was alone, I dropped my head in my arms and cried.

* * *

Lily didn't waste any time getting organized. She gave her landlord one month's notice and started packing. I dreaded the day she was supposed to move in and I wrecked my entire Christmas holidays worrying about it, especially when Dad started talking about how living with Lily would mean we both had to be more considerate. And he was right.

Once Lily moved in, everything I'd always been allowed to do suddenly required permission. For the first time ever, Dad set house rules and the list grew every day. I wasn't allowed to play loud music or video games in the living room. I couldn't leave the toilet seat up. I had to check if it was okay to eat something in the fridge in case Lily was planning on using it for dinner the next night. I wasn't allowed to bring friends over after school because we might make a mess. I had to pick up after myself every evening before I went to bed. I was used to doing some of the housework, but suddenly, in addition to doing the dishes and vacuuming, I was given the job of scrubbing the bathroom every day, because Lily was a clean-freak and couldn't stand to see toothpaste spit in the sink. I couldn't wear my shoes inside and I found out quickly that if I left my schoolbag at the front door, Lily would call me lazy and make a funny growling noise in her throat.

Within a few weeks after she'd officially moved in, Dad and I started to argue and spent whole evenings not talking to each other. We had our first real fight one night after Vic and I left two empty cereal bowls in the kitchen sink. When Lily came home from work she complained, and even though I went straight out to the kitchen to wash and put the bowls away, she wouldn't let it go. The next thing I knew, Dad was in my bedroom.

"You know she doesn't like you to have friends over after school," he said wearily.

"It was just Vic. All we did was play X-Box. You used to like it when I had friends over after school so I wouldn't be alone. But now that Lily's here, you want me to sit by myself every day and not even breathe in case I mess up the air!" I knew I was exaggerating, but I'd had enough of Lily's complaining that I needed to "smarten up," "pick up," and "shut up."

"It stresses Lily out when she has to come home and clean up before she makes dinner. It's inconsiderate and you should know better."

"Dad, get real. It was *two* cereal bowls and *two* spoons. It's not like we trashed the place."

"I don't know what's gotten into you lately," he said hotly. "All we ever do is argue."

I felt my hands start to shake."Nothing's gotten into me!"I screamed. "It's Lily. I can't do anything without her freaking out. It's my place too, you know."

"Keep your voice down,"he bellowed suddenly. His voice was so loud I felt it vibrate inside my chest. I sank into the bed and stared blankly up at him.

"Look, I'm sorry I yelled," he said in a much quieter voice."This is a big adjustment for you *and* me. But it's a bigger adjustment for Lily. She's not used to living with two guys."

"What about Quan and Sang? She used to live with them,"I said. The anger in me had gone flat. Instead, I felt hurt and confused, even a little scared. Lily didn't take up much space physically, but she'd taken over our entire lives.

"That's different. Just try to be patient while we all adjust. I know it's not easy. But we've got to find a way to get along."

"That's just the thing. I'm making all the effort and she's not doing anything."

"Is that what you think?"

"Yeah, and she picks on me all the time too."

"Anything else?"

"She hogs the bathroom in the morning. Some days I have to wait and pee at school."

"I'll ask her to let you in first from now on,"he said and left abruptly.

That night I was upset about Dad yelling at me and I had a hard time falling asleep. Lily woke me at six the next morning so I could use the bathroom first, and I was so sleepy I thought it was eight. I had my shoes on and was heading out the door before I realized how early it was. That was the way it was with Lily. She always found a way to get back at me, while making it look as if she was trying to get along.

For the first few months after Lily moved in, our father-son Sundays were sacred and I had Dad to myself that one day a week. As soon as the snow melted we went to the ball diamond to practice. Lily spent those days alone in the apartment, writing home or watching TV. At first she said she liked the time to herself, but before long we started coming back to an icy silence – the apartment would be as cold as an igloo. That's when Dad invited her along. So the following Sunday we took her to the park to play catch, but she ducked whenever the ball came near her. Dad spent more time coaching her on how to hold the glove than throwing the ball. We tried Frisbee another Sunday, but she squealed when I accidentally hit her in the leg. As a special treat we even went to the city zoo, but ended up arguing about whether the animals were better off in the zoo or in the wild. I said the wild, but Lily said some of them would be extinct otherwise and that zoos served a purpose. Dad walked the barrier between us, not wanting to take sides. When things got awkward, he bought us ice cream.

I knew our Sundays had gone from guy-time to Lily-time – with me as the sidekick – when Dad suggested we go to the butterfly conservatory.

"You want to spend the afternoon looking at *butterflies*?" I asked incredulously.

"Yeah, Lily's been wanting to go since she got here, but she never had anyone to go with."

"Maybe I'll just skip it this week," I said as I pictured the two of them holding hands and giggling together, the way they did on the couch after dinner most nights.

I was hoping to hurt his feelings, but I wasn't expecting to feel so terrible about doing it. It was the first Sunday *ever* that we hadn't spent together. While they went off with hot coffee in a thermos and a bag of custard-filled donuts for the bus ride, I sat home alone.

When they came crashing back into the apartment five hours later, breathless, glowing, and promising to tell me some important news over diner, I wished like crazy that I'd gone along.

CHAPTER 5

After three years, they explained to me, Lily had finally saved enough money to send for Quan and Sang. She'd used the time alone with Dad, time that should have been mine, to plan it all out.

"We'll have to move before Quan and Sang arrive," she beamed. "This place isn't big enough for three boys."

The chicken I'd been chewing felt suddenly like sawdust and I had to wash it down quickly with water. I gulped and then gasped. "We're *all* going to live together?" I asked.

"We thought it would be nice, all of us together. That way we can help the twins adjust faster," Dad said.

I nodded and concentrated on breathing, but it was hard.

"We can start looking in the paper tonight," Dad suggested. "I'm sure we can find a good three-bedroom apartment. Any idea of where you'd like to live?" he asked me.

"I don't want to move. I like this apartment. We've been here since I was five," I managed to say.

"It'll be nice to move," Dad said cheerfully. "A bit more space would be good."

"We probably can't afford anything bigger," I mumbled.

"We won't know until we look," he said to me. Then he turned to Lily. "Why don't we go get a newspaper while Devon does the dishes?"

Lily grabbed her purse and they left. I grumbled to myself as I cleared the plates. *First Lily moves in, now Quan and Sang are coming. It's going to be three against two. Why can't he see what's happening? What does he even like about her?*

I stopped in the middle of washing the glasses and called Vic.

"I can't believe we're all going to live together. I can't believe we have to move!" I said.

"Don't stress so much – people move all the time. Just don't let them move you to another neighborhood."

"But I'm going to have to live with Lily's kids!"

"Hey, I have to put up with my brothers all the time."

"That's different. You grew up with them. You're related. These guys don't even speak English."

"Eric has to live with his step-sister and he manages okay."

"This is different. I've never even met them."

"You need to chill, Dev. You'll get used to it. You've just had it too good, that's all."

"Whatever," I said before saying goodbye and hanging up, feeling more frustrated than before.

When Dad and Lily returned, they sat together looking at the apartment-for-rent ads – or at least Dad looked at the ads and read them aloud. Lily either nodded or scowled.

"Three-bedroom townhouse, finished rec room in basement, and it's close to Devon's school?" Dad offered.

"That sounds good. Quan and Sang can have the bedrooms upstairs, and Devon can have the basement all to himself maybe?"

She made it sound like a privilege, but I suspected she was trying to get me as far away as possible. It wasn't enough that she'd come between me and Dad and got us fighting, she wanted me physically removed as well. She probably would have liked it if I disappeared altogether, but since I didn't have a mother or any other family, she was stuck with me.

"That might be good, hey Dev?" Dad asked.

"I dunno. Maybe." I was feeling too stubborn to say what I was really thinking.

"Is it in our price range?" Lily asked.

"It's a bit of a stretch, but it would be nice not to have someone above us for once." Dad smiled.

"Let's call and then go look tomorrow," Lily said as she clapped her hands together.

All through dinner the next night I kept my head down and blinked back tears. While I chewed silently, Dad and Lily talked about what the townhouse would be like. Because I didn't share their excitement, I felt like an outsider, and by the time we left for the appointment with the landlord, my stomach was twisted in knots.

The townhouse was at the back of the railway tracks and across from an industrial area. As soon as we walked in, I knew Lily would love it. Compared to our apartment, it was clean, big, and modern. There was a large kitchen and living room on the main floor, three bedrooms and a bathroom on the top floor, and a rec room and laundry room in the basement.

Lily gasped when she saw the size of the kitchen.

"Look! So much room. I can cook for ten! And there's space for everyone to eat at once."

I wandered down to the basement to get away from her happiness. The room was cool and dark, which matched my mood. There was only one small window at the far end. I was standing on my tiptoes looking out of the window when Dad came down.

"What do you think?" he asked hopefully.

"It's kind of dark."

"There's plenty of space though."

"Yeah, I guess. But I'd be pretty far away from you."

"It seems farther than it is. I bet if you yelled, I could still hear you. Besides, you won't be down here all the time. Hey, did you see the back deck? We'll be able to have barbecues outside during the summer. And there's a huge parking lot across the street that will be perfect for skate-boarding."

I nodded. I wanted to be agreeable. But it was hard.

"At least you could have some privacy down here."

"I guess," I said, thinking that being two floors away from Quan and Sang might be a good thing. After all, I had no idea what to expect. I knew only that they had just turned thirteen, were twins, and were Vietnamese. I had no idea if we would have anything in common or would even get along. The idea of sharing my life with two more strangers terrified me.

Dad broke through my thoughts. "You haven't said what you think yet."

"Would I be able to have Vic and the guys over if we stayed down here – without Lily freaking out?"

"Of course."

"Do you promise to come down and visit?" I asked.

"Of course. I'll come down every night. We can set up the X-Box and hang out together."

"Just you and me?"

"Just you and me. It'll be our spot."

"And Lily won't bug us?"

"Of course not – you'll be the boss down here. You'll see," he said and pulled me into a bear hug.

The hug felt good, but even though I knew he meant to reassure me, I didn't stop worrying. This wasn't going to be a simple move – it was going to be a whole new life and I still wanted my old one back.

CHAPTER 6

From the day Lily made her big announcement, my stomach ached, and whenever I thought about the twins, it got worse. Sometimes when Dad and Lily were still at work, I'd stare at the picture of the twins that Lily had hanging on the living room wall. From one angle I thought they looked kind and from another I thought they looked mean. Luckily, turning twelve, studying for my year-end tests and packing up the apartment took up a lot of time, which meant I didn't get as much time to worry about their upcoming arrival.

We moved into the townhouse on a crazy-hot day in the middle of summer, just two weeks before the twins arrived. Vic, Eric, and Cody came to help, and we sweated as we carried box after box inside. By the middle of the afternoon, our T-shirts were completely soaked. We had a water gun fight in the backyard to cool down. Lily unpacked and told us where to put things, while Dad unloaded the heaviest boxes. The guys had fun seeing who could carry the biggest stuff, and they didn't seem to mind how bossy Lily was. But I hated the way she ordered us all around like a bunch of slaves.

When we were finally settled, Lily had Dad paint the twins' rooms: blue for Quan and green for Sang. They bought beds and desks at a second-hand store down the street and they got new bedding and blinds at the department store downtown. Then Lily fussed over their rooms as the big day drew closer. She shifted pencils and books on their desks, straightened their blankets and pillows. She stood at their doorways and wiped tears from her eyes each night before going to bed.

"They've never had their own beds. They've always shared with me or their grandparents. They won't believe all of this is for them," she said.

33

Dad must have found her tears sweet or something but when I saw her cuddling up to him in front of Sang's room, I felt like throwing up. I hated her emotional displays because they seemed so fake. She claimed to love kids, but she didn't like me or my friends at all.

When Dad finished painting the twins' rooms, he painted the rec room red for me – just like my old bedroom had been. He said he wanted to make me feel at home, but I knew he didn't want me to feel left out. He bought me new bedding and lamps too, and later I heard Lily accuse him of spoiling me.

As he promised, Dad came down to my room every night and we talked while we played Star Wars on the X-Box. The game was totally ancient, but it was Dad's favorite. During the last few days before they arrived, we talked mostly about Quan and Sang.

"Bringing two families together is never easy, but this is going to be even more difficult since the twins speak very little English," Dad said.

"I hope you don't expect me to entertain them all the time. I still want to hang out with my friends. I've hardly even seen Vic this summer because we've been so busy packing and unpacking."

"We don't expect you to give up your friends. Just get the twins used to school when it starts. Show them around. Maybe eat lunch with them. They're going to be completely lost for a while."

"What if they can't keep up at school?"

"The school will test them before placing them. And they'll take extra English classes in the afternoons. I'm sure they'll catch on."

"Lily's going to be even fussier now," I complained. "I'll have to be 'considerate' of her *and* of them."

"We're all going to need some space and time to get used to each other. But in a few months, things will be more settled. You'll see."

"That's what you always say: *you'll see*," I said.

"And have I been wrong?" he asked and nudged my shoulder playfully.

I knew he wanted me to smile, to give him some sign that I thought everything was going to be okay. That's when I realized he was just as nervous as I was. I wanted to ask him if he ever wished it was just the two of us again.

He looked at his watch and stood up. "Well, I guess I should get to bed," he said. "We have to get up early tomorrow. The boys are already in the air, halfway here."

"Yeah, it's going to be a long day."

"By the way, Lily asked if you'd mind staying home while we go get the twins. The taxi's going to be crowded with the four of us, and she thought it might be less overwhelming if they meet us one at a time."

I was hurt to be excluded, but I didn't want to let on. It seemed to me that every time something big was about to happen, Lily found a way to sideline me.

"That's okay. I understand," I said. "I'd rather sleep in anyway."

"Yeah, they should outlaw six a.m. arrivals. Sleep tight," Dad said before he ruffled my hair and headed back upstairs.

I slept restlessly that night, and the next morning when I heard Lily and Dad moving around upstairs, I was too tired to go up and say goodbye. Before they left, Dad came down and touched my shoulder.

"Devon? You awake?"

"Yeah, just lying here."

"We're going now."

"Okay. See you when you get back," I said groggily.

"It's going to work out fine. Really, you'll see," he said.

He waited for me to respond, but I was out of words.

When I heard the front door close I got out of bed, went upstairs, and wandered around the townhouse. It seemed so big when I was alone, but I knew it wouldn't feel that way when there were five people living in it. I looked in every room, in every corner, in every drawer. Quan's and Sang's drawers were empty except for a few pieces of clothing Lily had bought. I wondered if they'd like what she'd picked out and how they felt about moving to the United States. I wondered what they thought about becoming part of a new family, what they felt about me. I tried to keep calm. Next I went through the bathroom drawers and saw more soaps and creams than Dad and I'd ever used in our lifetimes. In the kitchen I examined the strange tea leaves and packets of dried herbs that were labeled in Vietnamese handwriting. I looked around the living room and took a deep breath. Then I went downstairs to wait and to hope it wasn't going to be as bad as I was expecting.

CHAPTER 7

When they arrived home from the airport, the first thing I noticed from downstairs was the sound of the twins and Lily speaking Vietnamese together. I'd heard Lily speak it on the phone, but I'd never before heard her in a two-way conversation. They barely even took a breath between sentences.

I dreaded the first meeting because it was going to make my new life real. I also dreaded how Lily was going to treat me in front of the twins. So I waited for what seemed like the happiest moment to join in, then climbed the stairs slowly. I held onto the doorknob for a few moments before I finally pushed it open and stepped into the kitchen.

Quan and Sang were sitting at the table looking down at their cutlery, and the first thing I noticed was the identical parts in their hair. Lily was frying sausages and Dad was putting bread in the toaster. Nobody noticed me. It was as if I didn't exist.

Finally Dad looked up and smiled.

"Ah, Devon! You're awake. Come and meet Quan and Sang."

I stepped toward the table and the twins looked up at me curiously. Lily said something in Vietnamese, and I thought I saw their expressions harden. Then in English she spoke slowly.

"Quan, Sang, this is Devon."

They were wearing khaki pants and long-sleeved shirts – in the heat of summer – but they hadn't broken a sweat. They nodded, and I forced a smile to my face. She spoke again in Vietnamese and they held out their hands for me to shake. I was surprised, but I took Quan's hand first, then Sang's. There was no feeling in their handshakes.

Lily gestured at me, then the basement door. She spoke in Vietnamese and I was sure she'd said something mean, but before I could say anything, Dad spoke up.

"Come and have some breakfast, Dev."

He pulled out a chair for me, and I sat down and opened a box of cereal while Quan and Sang watched. I smiled at them, but their expressions didn't change.

"Uh, how was your flight?" I asked.

They just stared at me until Lily spoke to them in Vietnamese.

Then Quan spoke slowly, "Good. Thank you." Sang didn't reply at all.

"Their plane arrived right on time," Dad said to fill the uncomfortable silence.

"That's good," I muttered with my mouth half full.

Lily scowled at me.

"*Tóc hung hung đỏ,*" she said harshly to the twins.

The boys looked at her, then at me, and then at each other again. I knew she was criticizing me, and I couldn't stand her talking about me when I was in the same room. I couldn't help myself, I had to say something.

"What did you say?"

"Nothing important."

"But I want to know. What did you say?"

"Why? Are you going to learn Vietnamese?"

"Maybe," I said.

"I just told them what your dad said. You're very nosey today."

Lily and I stared at each other. Quan and Sang stared down at the table.

"So what should we all do today?" Dad asked.

He had come over to stand behind me, and he put his hands on my shoulders. I felt relieved, as if someone was volunteering to be on my team, even though we were probably going to lose.

"We could go to the pool," I offered lamely. "It's supposed to get really hot later."

"No. We'll rest," Lily said. "Tomorrow we'll take the boys to see their new school." She spoke with so much authority there was no room to argue. Then she switched to Vietnamese and both boys left the table.

"They need to wash and to sleep now," Lily said as she disappeared up the stairs behind them.

Dad and I looked at each other but didn't speak. We finished eating and shared sections of the newspaper: sports for him and the comics for me. It was quiet upstairs and, for a moment, I imagined Lily had never come into our lives.

Finally, Dad looked up and cleared his throat.

"I'm worried about how you're coping with so much change."

"It's a little late to ask now, don't you think?" I asked.

"Just promise you'll talk to me. We can get through anything if we stick together."

"Okay, I promise. But didn't you hear how she spoke to me? I just know she was saying something bad about me."

"How do you know?"

"Her tone ... I just know."

"Look, she's tired and stressed out. Let's try not to make too much of it today. Okay?"

He shook the newspaper and started reading again.

So much for sticking together, I thought, before heading back downstairs.

CHAPTER 8

Before we left for the first day of school, Lily gave us strict instructions in both English and Vietnamese.

"Take them straight to the office. The Principal is expecting them. They have to be enrolled in the right grade first thing. And don't forget to bring them home after school."

"I won't forget," I said with a scowl.

"Thanks for helping out," Dad said. "It'll only be for the first few days."

"I wish I was taking them," Lily said spitefully. "The boss won't even give me one morning off."

"Devon will take good care of them. Won't you, Devon?"

I was sitting on the front steps, and I nodded while Dad patted Sang on the back. Sang looked nervously at Quan.

"We will be good," Quan said.

Lily kissed both boys, Dad gave me a quick hug, then he and Lily walked toward the bus stop, with Lily looking back every few steps. When they disappeared around the corner the twins looked at me. It was the first time we'd been alone since they arrived two weeks earlier.

"Uh, well, we still have a bit of time. We don't have to be there until eight-thirty." I spoke slowly and showed them the time on my watch.

They both nodded and when they sat down beside me I suddenly suspected they understood more English than they let on.

"It's a pretty good school. We have a good track team. I was on it last year. Do you like sports?"

Quan shook his head.

"Video games?"

He shook his head again.

"What did you do in Vietnam?"

"School and work," he said.

"There must be something you like to."

"*Co tuong*," Sang said brightly, even though Quan was glaring at him.

"What's that?"

"Vietnamese chess."

"The game? Chess? You play?"

Sang nodded.

"Well, there you go. There's a chess club at our school. Maybe you can join. "

Sang nodded, but Quan didn't respond. I looked at my watch again. "Maybe we should get going."

We grabbed our school bags and headed down the street. Normally I met up with Vic and rode my skateboard to school, but that morning I walked so Quan and Sang could keep up. As we got closer, I started to see kids I recognized.

"Hey, Dev!"

I turned around when I heard Vic's voice. He was barreling toward us on his skateboard.

"This must be Quan and Sang?" he said, then grabbed his skateboard and walked with us.

I nodded.

"How's it going?" he said to them.

"Good. Thank you. It is nice to meet you," Quan said.

"Yeah, cool to meet you too. I hope Devon's being a good tour guide," he said, smirking.

"How are they doing?" he whispered a moment later.

"I dunno, they don't speak much English."

He glanced at them and then asked me. "Are you allowed to skateboard after school or do you have to babysit?"

"I have to get them home until they know the way. But I think they have an after-school English class, so we could do a few tricks in the teacher's parking lot. I don't have my board with me though."

"That's okay. We can take turns with mine. Hey, I hope we get the same classes this year."

"Me too. I'll find you after homeroom. I just have to get them to the principal's office, then I'm free."

By then we'd reached the school, so Vic dropped his skateboard on the sidewalk and took off.

"See you in a few," he called back.

I led Quan and Sang through the front doors and into the principal's office.

The secretary looked up and smiled.

"Hello, Devon!" she said brightly. "Did you have a good summer?"

"It was okay. You?"

"Yes, thanks for asking. My grandchildren came to visit from Oregon."

"Nice. Is Mr. Morely here? I'm supposed to bring Quan and Sang to him first thing." I motioned at the twins who were standing close beside me.

"You leave them here with me and find your class before the bell rings." She stood up and ushered the twins to a row of chairs.

I said bye, then ducked out. When I glanced back, the twins were looking scared, standing side-by-side with their backpacks squarely on their backs like a couple of pre-schoolers. I almost went back to check that they would be okay, but the warning bell rang. So I scrambled down the hall to find my homeroom.

I didn't see Quan and Sang again until lunchtime. I found them in the cafeteria, sitting at a corner table by themselves eating the lunches Lily had packed for them. They were holding their sandwiches tightly with both hands.

"Hi," I said. "How's your day going?"

"Good," Quan said, but Sang didn't speak.

"Is it okay if Vic and I join you?"

Quan nodded, and Vic and I sat down.

I unwrapped my sandwich and started to eat. At first we didn't talk, but then Vic started to complain about his summer and how bored he was at the swim camp his mother had made him go to. I told him he was lucky he got to swim every day, and he told me I was lucky I got to sleep in a basement and have some privacy. He had to share a third-floor bedroom.

"I cooked up there," he said. "I felt like a roast chicken every morning," he said.

"Yeah, but you look more like a roast pig," I said and laughed.

I glanced at Quan and Sang and they weren't laughing, but I didn't bother trying to explain. When they finished eating, they excused themselves.

"Where're you going?" I asked, suddenly feeling guilty.

"To the library to study," Quan said.

"Okay, I'll meet you in the parking lot after school and walk you home."

"Thank you," Quan said.

As soon as they were out of earshot, Vic spoke.

"Talk about keeners. I don't plan on doing any homework until at least October."

"That's why your marks suck," I joked.

The day went quickly and I didn't see Quan or Sang again until I was in the parking lot with Vic. I suddenly noticed them watching us.

"Hey there. Are you guys ready?"

Quan nodded and Sang looked down at his shoes.

"See you later, Vic," I said and headed down the street with the twins behind me.

"So how was your afternoon?" I asked as we walked.

"Good," Quan said.

"How was your English class?"

"Good," Quan said again.

They didn't say anything else, and I gave up trying to start a conversation.

"You guys want a snack?" I asked when we got inside.

They shook their heads and started up the stairs with their backpacks still on their backs.

"Wait," I said and reached for my backpack, which I had left by the door. "Most guys just sling it over their shoulder like this. See?"

I showed them and they nodded. Then I reached toward Sang to mess up his hair a bit. He flinched.

"It's okay, I just wanted to fix your hair."

I reached out again and ruffled the front so that it hung in his eyes a little and hid the careful part. He reached up to feel it, then turned and followed Quan upstairs.

"Thank you," he called back down.

* * *

When Dad and Lily came home that night, I half expected Lily to thank me for helping the twins through their first day of school. But she flew past where I was sitting at the kitchen table and called out for them. They came down the stairs quietly and kissed her cheek. She inspected them, hugged them, then brushed Sang's hair out of his eyes while she spoke to him harshly in Vietnamese. He looked embarrassed but didn't answer. I would have died if I were him. But he didn't complain. Neither of them ever complained or talked back. In comparison I was rude and ungrateful, mouthy even. I overheard Dad try to explain me to Lily later.

"It's just a cultural difference. We don't expect utter obedience from our children here – we encourage individuality."

"You want kids to talk back?" she asked.

"Not exactly. We don't want them to talk back just for the sake of arguing, but I want Devon to learn how to think for himself."

"It's your own fault then, when he doesn't listen."

"Devon is respectful, but he's ... spirited. His temperament matches his hair," Dad said as he chuckled.

"Spirited, ha! He's spoiled and he's a bad influence on Quan and Sang."

"If Quan and Sang become a little more outspoken, it won't be Devon's fault, and it won't be a bad thing," he said sharply.

It was the first time I heard him speak so sternly to Lily, and I could hear her fuming from around the corner. She made a different noise for every emotion. She clicked her tongue for sympathy, she snorted when she disagreed, and she made a low growl deep in her throat when she fumed. She growled like a lion right then and I shuddered.

CHAPTER 9

By early November Quan and Sang were getting to and from school on their own, and I was staying late two afternoons a week for basketball practice. I was also hanging out more at Vic's. When I *was* home, I spent most of my time downstairs unless I was eating or using the bathroom. Because Dad was working extra hours, I didn't see him at all some days, or only a few minutes a night when he came down to play a quick game on my X-Box. If I'd been spending more time with him, I might have noticed how tired he was.

As it was, I didn't realize he was sick until the Christmas holidays when we were home together for a few days. That's when I noticed how often he fell asleep on the couch and that he never felt like eating. At first, I didn't think much of it, but then he started to look pale and yellow. He blamed it on the weather and the extra hours at work. But then he started to get a pain on his right side. That's when he let on how bad he'd really been feeling – that's when I started to worry.

Lily told him his liver was "acting up" and that he needed to drink more green tea. She made him a special remedy to fight the infection she imagined was raging inside him, and Dad, who always went along with her ideas, drank cup after cup of green tea packed with "milk thistle" and a bunch of other strange-looking powders she stockpiled in the cupboard above the fridge.

But Lily's tea didn't help Dad get better – instead, he got worse. The pain got so bad that he ended up in the emergency room one weekend at the end of February. He laid doubled-up on the narrow hospital bed. I knew the pain must be bad to twist him up the way it did. I stood by him and listened to Lily vent about "Western" doctors.

44

"Going to the doctor here is like having a baby try to cure you. They ignore a thousand years of medical wisdom. They poison you and then wonder why you don't get better. The fools."

I didn't bother to point out that her remedies hadn't helped either.

The emergency room doctor found elevated levels of some kind of enzymes in Dad's blood, which, like Lily said, meant there was a problem with his liver. They asked him a million questions about his lifestyle: how much alcohol he drank, if he'd ever had hepatitis, if he took drugs, if he'd ever had an alcohol addiction, if he suffered from any chronic pain, or if he had been taking any pain pills recently. I didn't like the questions or the doctor's tone of voice, and when I couldn't stand it any longer, I interrupted.

"My dad doesn't take drugs. He barely even drinks alcohol. Why don't you figure out what's wrong with him instead of accusing him of doing something wrong."

Dad put his hand on mine. "It's okay Devon, they're routine questions. Right doctor?"

"That's right. I'm just taking his history," the doctor agreed, but I noticed his tone changed.

When the doctor left, Lily fumed some more.

"They're wasting our time. They'll kill you before they cure you."

"What do you know?" I asked. "Are you a doctor? Have you ever even been to a doctor here?" My voice was a little too loud and even I cringed at how rude I sounded.

"My Uncle Tho is a very wise doctor. I learned from him," she said and glared at me.

"Listen, Devon, can you find me a bottle of water? My mouth feels like sandpaper," Dad asked gently.

I jammed my hands in my pockets and walked away.

When I came back, Dad was pulling on his boots and trying his best to smile.

"Has the doctor been back?" I asked.

Dad nodded, and Lily leaned down to tie his laces.

"What did he say?" I asked.

"He said I'm going to need to take it easy – probably for a couple of months. For now I have to drink plenty of fluids, get lots of rest, and go for more tests."

"What kind of tests?"

"Blood tests. Urine tests. Liver tests. Routine stuff. Nothing to worry about. Let's go home."

I knew he was lying, but I didn't press him for details. I wanted to get him out of the hospital and away from that doctor.

Back at home Lily set Dad up on the couch and sent me running for every little thing he could possibly want: a heating pad for his back, an extra pillow for his head, another blanket to keep him warm. When I went to the kitchen to make him some toast, Lily was brewing him another cup of tea.

"What's in that, anyway?" I asked.

"Milk thistle, ginger, and extra ginkgo. He needs more energy," she said and then turned her back on me.

"Are you sure all that stuff is good for him?"

She turned and looked at me so hard I wondered if she had x-ray vision or something. But she didn't say a word.

When I couldn't stand it a second longer, I went to check on Dad. He'd fallen asleep, so I sat on the floor beside him and listened to his ragged breathing. I heard the twins upstairs, the toilet flush, a train rumble past. Then I heard Lily pick up the phone and dial.

"Hello. Can I speak to your father?" she asked, then paused.

"Jack? It's Lily. Bryce and I are both sick. We won't be in for a few days." She paused again.

"I know, but I don't think you want us passing this around." She paused, faked a cough, and blew her nose. "I'll call you tomorrow."

A gloomy silence filled the room when Lily hung up. We both knew their boss was a jerk about anyone taking days off.

"I've only got three sick days left this year," Dad said quietly. I was surprised he was awake.

"The doctor said you need to rest, so don't worry about work," Lily said as she rushed in from the kitchen and handed him the cup of tea.

"I can't take off for a few days and especially not for a couple of months. I'll get fired and we won't make rent."

"You should worry less and think about getting better more. You've worked there ten years. They won't fire you for being sick and going for a few tests," she said and made her fuming noise.

"They can and they will," Dad said.

"I'll talk to them and explain it's temporary. They'll understand when I'm through."

Dad ran his hand over his hair and looked up at the ceiling.

"Can I get you anything?" I asked.

"He needs to rest, so stop pestering him," Lily said.

"I'm okay," he whispered and squeezed my hand.

Lily snorted her disapproval and left, but Dad and I ignored her.

"They'll figure it out soon and help you get better," I said as I leaned over for a hug.

He put his arms around me and I was shocked to feel him trembling.

CHAPTER 10

The next day when I got home from school, Lily was doing laundry. She came to my room and looked me up and down. I felt my legs go weak.

"What?" I asked.

She cleared her throat. "There's a part-time job opening up at the meat works. I told them you'd take it."

It was not a suggestion. I started freaking out inside. It wasn't that I was afraid of working. I'd had part-time jobs before: shoveling driveways, raking leaves, painting porches. The summer I was ten I'd even walked a neighbor's dog every afternoon so I could buy the X-Box. But having Lily line up a job for me at the slaughterhouse of all places was terrifying.

"What?" I asked again.

"*Ngu như lừa!*" she said, slipping into Vietnamese the way she'd started to lately whenever she was upset. "You start working next week. Three hours each night. You can clean the floors, dust the office. Bring old clothes."

I couldn't find any words, though there were plenty of thoughts screaming inside my head. I finally managed to ask, "Why me?"

"Because otherwise we won't have enough money to pay the rent. I can't pay everything myself."

"What about Quan and Sang? Why don't you get them a job?"

"They study and you never study. You're never even grateful. It's time you learned how to work."

"I'm not ungrateful," I protested.

"You're ungrateful and spoiled and now you can pay some bills," she said.

"Does Dad know about this?"

"No, but you will tell him tonight. Say it's your idea."

"Why would I do that?"

"Because he'll worry himself more sick if you don't. Do you want him to die?"

I hated her for even suggesting such a thing. "Okay, but just until he gets better. And I think Quan and Sang should help out too."

"You're not the boss. I say when Quan and Sang are ready to work."

She jabbed me hard in the chest with her finger, then turned to leave. She paused only long enough to say, "Come up in ten minutes."

When she left, I sat down on my bed and tried to stop my head from spinning. I dreaded the thought of working at the slaughterhouse, yet I knew money was tight and I didn't want to get kicked out of the townhouse. I also didn't want Dad to worry. I knew he'd say "no way" if I didn't play along. He'd never even let me inside the meat works building before.

Finally, I scraped together enough energy to go upstairs. Dad was watching the news.

"Do you need anything?" I asked and sat down next him.

"I'm okay."

"Uh, listen. I was thinking about getting a part-time job."

I could see Lily watching me from the kitchen.

"What?" he asked as he shifted his full attention to me.

"I was thinking of getting a job – like after school and on weekends. I'm getting good grades and, well, I know it would help pay a few bills – just until you get back to work."

"It's nice of you to offer, Devon, really. But we'll be okay. I've got a bit of savings to get us through."

"Really?" I asked, but then I saw Lily glaring at me. "I mean, we should keep our savings safe, you know? A few hours a day won't kill me, and I've got an easy semester."

"Where are you going to get a job? You're only twelve years old."

That's when Lily made her grand entrance.

"Devon! What a good idea! Maybe we can find something at the meat works. We're shorthanded."

"Absolutely not! He's not working there," Dad said with as much energy as he'd shown in weeks.

"Not with the animals," she said. "Just office work. I've got too much to do. He can come and help me."

"I dunno," Dad said, shaking his head.

"It'll be okay," I said. "It's not like I'd be working a whole shift." I tried to sound convincing.

"But he's too young," Dad said to Lily.

"He'll be thirteen in a few months. The boss's son worked there last summer and he was only thirteen. We won't put his name on the payroll."

Dad turned to me. "Okay. A couple of hours a day, but *only* if you promise not to go in the back. That's no place for a boy. And if your grades start to slip, then you're through."

"I'll be fine, don't worry," I said. I looked away from the smile of satisfaction on Lily's face.

CHAPTER 11

My job started that Monday. Vic complained that I couldn't hang out with him after school, but he walked me to the bus stop anyway.

"How long are you going to have this job?" he asked when the cross-city bus pulled up.

"Not long, maybe just a couple of months," I said.

"Still, it sucks that you have to work *every* night."

"I know," I said and climbed on.

The bus was almost full, but I found a seat near the back. While I rode, I ate the extra sandwich Lily packed and I did my homework. It took forty minutes to get across the city to where a last few businesses butted up against farms and fields.

The meat works was a series of low metal buildings surrounded by fenced holding areas and parking lots. When I got close I could smell the stench of cow manure. I ducked my head down into my winter coat so I wouldn't have to breathe in the rotten air.

Lily was the only one in the front office when I arrived. She was sitting behind the counter, typing on a computer. She glanced up when I walked through the door, but then she looked down again when she saw it was me. I looked out the front window while I waited for her to tell me what to do.

"Change into your old clothes. And here. Wear these over top," she said after a couple of minutes. She'd thrown me a pair of coveralls.

"There's a washroom through there." She pointed at a door that led to the back of the building. I hesitated, remembering that Dad said I shouldn't go where the animals were butchered.

"Would you rather change here in front of me?" she asked when I didn't move.

I shook my head.

"Then hurry up and stop being such a baby," she said sharply. "No animals are back there."

I leaned into the heavy metal door and swallowed the lump in my throat. The first thing I saw when I looked past the door were hooks hanging from the ceiling and a cement floor wet with blood. The first thing I smelled was raw meat. My stomach heaved. I covered my mouth with my hand and ran to the restroom, relieved that nobody was there to hear my sandwich splash into the toilet. When my stomach settled, I rinsed my mouth and pulled on the baggy coveralls.

"You take more time to change than a girl," Lily said impatiently when I returned.

"Well, I'm here now," I scowled.

She led me back to the quartering room.

"It's not rocket science. Just get the floor clean," she demanded.

She motioned to the hoses, brooms, and wide rubber squeegees leaning in the corner. I wanted to move, but my legs wouldn't budge. I finally understood what Lily had in mind. There was no office cleaning to do, there was no computer work that needed attention. Lily expected me to scrub the floor. I was so angry I could barely think. I wanted to walk straight past her and catch a bus home – go tell Dad exactly what was happening. But I knew she'd find a way to make me look bad. What I had to do, I decided, was suck it up and when Dad was better, tell him everything. Then he'd be so angry, it would be the end of Lily in our lives.

"There. Wash the floors and push the dirty water down the drain. Go. We have to leave by seven-thirty."

She gave me a shove and I stumbled forward. It took all the energy I had to keep from shaking. I reached for a hose and pressed the trigger. Then I blinked back tears as I watched the blood and clots of fat flowing across the floor.

Lily watched me work for a few minutes then disappeared. When she left, I looked around. I tried to figure out how long it would take me to wash a floor the size of the school gym but I had no way of judging. I just knew the sooner I got finished, the sooner I could go home.

I worked steady and within an hour my arms ached. Lily never came to check up on me, so I was alone – except for when two men walked across the far end of the room and stopped to watch me before continuing on. I wondered if they were friends of Dad's and if they knew who I was.

Lily reappeared at the end of the night and sent me back to the restroom to change.

"Take a shower and be quick. We leave in five minutes," she said before the door closed behind me.

I peeled off my bloody coveralls and threw them in a laundry bin. Then I stripped naked and stepped into the showers where, until recently, I imagined Dad stood each afternoon and cleaned himself of the same filth. The hot water ran over my head, and I watched the red water swirl down the drain. I felt my stomach clench again, but I knew I had nothing more to throw up. I pumped a handful of soap from the dispenser and lathered my entire body, hoping to get rid of the smell as well as the blood.

"Devon. *Hurry up!* We have to go *now* or we'll miss the bus," Lily yelled into the restroom.

"Hang on," I said, drying myself quickly and pulling on my school clothes.

I shoved past her on my way out the front door. She looked at me with a curious expression but didn't say a word. Then I gulped back the winter air and stormed to the bus stop without waiting.

Lily sat beside me on the bus but we didn't speak. I fell asleep with my head against the window and when we arrived at our stop, she elbowed me.

"It's our stop. When we get inside, tell your dad you worked on a database today."

I didn't say a word. I just trudged along the sidewalk. My schoolbag felt like fifty pounds on my shoulder.

Once inside, we found Dad in the kitchen frying bacon. The smell made me want to puke yet again. Lily shooed him back to the couch.

"You need to rest. You shouldn't be in the kitchen. Where are Quan and Sang? They can cook if you're hungry."

"They went upstairs to study – I was just making you some sandwiches. You shouldn't have to work ten hours and cook too."

Lily pushed him all the way to the living room.

"You sit and talk with Devon."

I was surprised and wondered if she'd treat me better now that I was working. But somehow I knew she was just making time for me to lie to Dad and there was nothing I could ever do that would make her be nice to me.

CHAPTER 12

The day Dad got the results from his final round of tests, he came down to my bedroom. It was almost four weeks after I'd started my job at the meat works, but it felt like much longer. He sat down beside me and wiped the hair out of my eyes.

"You need a haircut soon."

"I'm growing it long, but maybe I can get the front trimmed Saturday when I finish work."

"I'm sorry, Devon. You're working too hard for a boy."

"I'm okay. I'm almost thirteen, remember? Anyway, stop worrying about me and just get better."

"That's what I came down to talk to you about."

"What?"

"Well, the doctors don't think my liver *will* get better. They think the damage is too serious. They don't know why it started to deteriorate so suddenly, but it might be hereditary. All they really know is that it's not cancer."

"But there must be more tests they can do, and when they figure it out they can help."

"I don't think they *can* figure it out. I think they've done every test there is."

"But I thought you said they still had another specialist for you to see."

"There will always be another specialist. But I think the truth is, they're stumped. At this point they can't even say how long my liver is going to last."

Suddenly an idea so terrible and sinister formed in my mind I couldn't help blurting it out.

"Do you think it's Lily?"

"What do you mean, *do I think it's Lily*?" he asked quickly.

"Do you think she's poisoning you? I mean, maybe that stuff she puts in your tea is bad for you. Did you tell the doctors what you've been drinking? Did you tell them about all that ginkgo thistle and stuff?"

The words tumbled out of my mouth. Dad shook his head sadly.

"I know you want to blame someone ... it's natural. But all Lily is trying to do is help. I don't know if milk thistle or ginkgo really works, but it's worth a shot. They say I'm a medical mystery." He stopped to catch his breath.

"No, seriously, think about it," I said. "You were healthy until you started drinking all that tea." The more I thought about what I was saying, the more convinced I was that Lily was somehow poisoning him. "Maybe she doesn't know what she's doing, even if her uncle did teach her. Maybe you should stop drinking it for a little while," I said.

"Don't be silly. It's just some dried herbs. It's not hurting me. It may not be helping, but it's not making me sick. I promise," he said and looked at me so sadly, I held back saying anything more.

"Anyhow, listen – I came down because I want to talk to you about something important."

I really hoped he wasn't going to start talking about what would happen if he died because I knew I'd burst into tears. Although I understood he was very sick, I couldn't stand thinking about what could happen.

"The best they can offer me is a liver transplant and they've put me on the waiting list. But the list is long and I may not have enough time. Lily wants to take me to Vietnam. She thinks her uncle can cure me – he can do stuff they don't do here. She's been on the phone home all week."

"You want to go all the way to *Vietnam*? You want to risk missing a transplant to take a chance on some Vietnamese herbs? Is her uncle even a real doctor?"

"I don't want to go, but I don't think there's a better option. The chance of me getting a transplant before my liver completely shuts down is remote. Lily's uncle might be my last chance. And yes, he's a real doctor."

"Isn't it expensive to fly all the way to Vietnam?"

"I've got enough savings to get us there and back and for a few weeks' stay while her uncle treats me. Eastern medicine is based on thousands of years of practice and even though we don't accept some of their ideas over here, they have a very high success rate in stopping liver disease and even in reversing some of the damage. I'm lucky to even have this chance."

"You're going to be gone for a few *weeks*?"

"*We're* going to be gone. I want you to come too. Quan and Sang can stay here with a friend of Lily's"

"What friend?" I was surprised to hear the sudden mention of a friend. We'd never met any of Lily's friends or heard her talk about any.

"A lady Lily stayed with when she first came from Vietnam is going to come and stay here. We can't afford five flights and Lily wants the boys to stay in school."

"What about school for me?"

"I'm sure your teachers can put some work together for you. I'll call and talk to Mr. Morely."

"When are we leaving?"

"As soon as we can get everything sorted out. Lily's looking into flights and visas. She already printed off passport applications for us. It's a lot to organize on short notice, but I think it can be done."

I didn't like the thought of flying all the way to Vietnam and staying with Lily's parents, but it was better than thinking about being away from Dad for so long.

"If you think it'll help, then I guess we have to try," I said and stood up.

"Where are you going?" Dad asked.

"I have to call Vic and tell him I might miss the track meet. He's going to be so mad. We wanted the same relay team as last year so we could kick butt again."

"Wait, Devon, before you get on the phone, you have to understand Lily's family is very poor. It won't be anything like living here. Vietnam is going to be a real change and Lily doesn't want you to be shocked when you see how they live."

I didn't say anything. I was too busy wondering why Lily was even letting me come on the trip in the first place and why she was leaving Quan and Sang behind.

CHAPTER 13

I had no idea there would be so much to do before our trip. I spoke to my teachers and by the end of the week I had a stack of assignments to bring with me. I made arrangements to take any tests when I returned, but I agreed to send assignments by email if I could find an Internet café, which Lily said would be possible. I only missed one day of school when Dad and I went in person to the passport office to rush the process, and I didn't miss a single shift at the meat works.

I'd never had a passport or been to a foreign country before, so even though the days leading up to our departure were hectic, I still found time to be nervous. I worried how I would stand not seeing my friends, how Dad would respond to the treatment from Lily's uncle, what it would be like to live in a country where I didn't speak the language, and how I would handle living with Lily's family in a tiny apartment. I was so nervous, in fact, that I spent three lunches in a row in the computer room at school, researching Ho Chi Minh City, where Lily's uncle and parents lived, and wishing I'd paid more attention that day at the library with Dad right after I'd first met Lily.

Vic and Cody found me on the third day watching video clips on YouTube. They leaned over my shoulder.

"Where's that?" Cody asked.

"Ho Chi Minh City, where we're going."

"Looks busy."

"Yeah, it does."

"Anything fun to do there?" he asked.

"I dunno," I said. "But, we're not going there to have fun. We're going to help my dad."

"Are you staying in here all lunch?" Vic asked.

"I'm almost done. Why?"

"Because it's actually warm outside for a change and we wanted to go out to the parking lot."

"Okay," I said. "I'll meet you there."

I knew they didn't believe me, but they wandered off and I tried another search.

Until I started to read up on Vietnam, the trip hadn't seemed real. I knew I'd be missing classes and track practices. I knew Vic and the guys didn't want me to go. But for some reason the idea hadn't completely sunk in. After I watched videos on YouTube of real people living in a real city so far away, I felt as if I was in a dream and everything was fuzzy. The days crumpled into one another and the closer we got to leaving, the more unreal it seemed.

Lily made most of the arrangements, and even though Dad managed to make a few calls, she organized our visas, the flights, transportation to and from the airports, and she also got some Vietnamese money out of the bank. Dad sent me to the doctor to get my immunizations updated, but Lily refused to get any herself or let Dad get them. Lily arranged a leave from work and hired a new temp to cover her, plus a high school kid to cover me. The boss surprised us and came by to wish Dad a good trip and a speedy recovery. He even delivered a get well card signed from everyone at work. We cleaned the house from top to bottom before we left so Lily's friend would feel comfortable, we paid all the bills, left money for groceries and packed our suitcases.

Lily put together a small bag for her and Dad and told me I'd have to pack light because there wasn't much room at her family's apartment. She allowed me one small backpack, but by the time I'd packed my schoolwork, there was little room left over. In the end I had only a few changes of clothes, some toiletries, two skateboarding magazines, a baseball cap, and a flashlight that I used to take camping when I was in cub scouts. At the last minute I unpinned a strip of photos from my bulletin board. They were a series of four that Dad and I had taken in a photobooth during one of our Sunday afternoons together, and I tucked them in the back of my wallet.

Less than three weeks after Dad told me about the trip, we were ready to go and I had to say goodbye to my friends. That was the hardest part. On my last night, I had them all over to play X-Box in the basement. I tried not to be sad, but it was hard not knowing how long I'd be away.

"So, you don't even know when you're coming back?"Vic asked for the fifth time, while he worked the controller.

"It'll depend on how my dad does. We have open-ended tickets."

"But is there a limit on when you have to come back by, before they, like, expire or something?" Eric asked.

"They're good for six months. Dad says we'll be gone a few weeks, but Lily says it'll be more like two months. Probably something in between."

"You could be gone two months! Are you kidding me? You get out of school for two months?" Cody asked enviously.

"It's not so great – I still have to do the work."

"Yeah, but you don't have to sit through Mrs. Lamba's math class," Vic said.

"Or Mr. Ahmad's civic studies." Eric rolled his eyes.

"You're going to miss your birthday,"Vic said sadly.

"I'm still going to have it."

"But not with us."

"I'll celebrate with you when I get back. We'll have our party then, when Dad's better."

"So what time does your flight leave?" Cody asked.

"Seven in the morning, but we have to be there two hours early. Lily has a taxi picking us up at four."

"That sucks," Cody said.

Eric glanced at his watch. "Whoa, you have to get up in, like, eight hours."

"We gotta go anyway,"Vic said when he crashed his podracer."Mom's meeting us outside at eight."

"Man, you totally suck at this game," I said.

"That's because it's from, like, five years ago."

"Not five years."

"Well, it's old anyway. I used to play it in, like, Grade Three," Vic complained.

"Liar," Cody said.

Vic grabbed his hoodie and pulled it over his head. The others jammed their feet into their shoes and we all tiptoed up the basement stairs so we wouldn't disturb Lily or Dad. Even though it was still early, the living room was dark and I opened the front door as quietly as I could.

"Have a good trip," Eric whispered as he slipped past me.

I nodded and fought the stinging in my eyes.

"Tell your dad bye for us," Cody called as he waved from the sidewalk.

"You better come back in time for the track meet," Vic warned before he ran to catch up to the others.

"Don't worry," I called out. "I'll be back before you know it."

I didn't believe it myself, but it seemed like the right thing to say.

CHAPTER 14

The flight to Vietnam was long and – despite the reason why we were flying to the other side of the world – exciting at the same time. I'd never been in an airport or on an airplane before. I loved the feel of the plane as it sped down the runway and lifted into the air. It was cool watching the city shrink below us. When the plane leveled off, I fiddled with the movie selections. I sat on one side of Dad and Lily sat on the other. Lily and I barely spoke, unless it was about something Dad needed. Sometimes when I glanced over at him sleeping, I would see her looking at him too. Our eyes would meet briefly, but I always looked away first.

Even though I was used to living in a city, Ho Chi Minh City was overwhelming. I walked through the airport in a daze, exhausted from the long flight. I followed Lily and Dad outside like a zombie. Lily waved down a taxi and settled on a price while I helped Dad into the backseat. A steady stream of cars flowed by and I didn't think we'd ever get a break, but the driver hit the accelerator and pulled into the line of traffic like he was in a video game. I braced for a crash, but cars only honked, then made room for us to squeeze in. The trip was slow and the driver stopped a lot. The congestion didn't seem to bother him at all and Lily didn't comment on it either, but I watched out the window the whole way. I'd never seen so much activity – so many cars, vans, motorbikes, and people streaming along the sidewalks. I couldn't stop staring at the mass of scooters; it was like a colony of ants swarming down the street. At one point we got stuck behind a lady pedaling a bicycle. She had a tall metal rack attached behind her seat and hanging from the rack were clear plastic bags puffed up with water and jumbo-sized goldfish.

We passed a walled courtyard with a fancy sand-coloured building set back in the distance and lined by a row of colorful flags. Later we passed a Kentucky Fried Chicken restaurant, which surprised me. There were signs with English words like Xerox and Citibank crammed beside signs with Vietnamese words that I couldn't read. We passed over a river and below there was a passenger ferry alongside a tugboat and several long, low, skinny boats filled with vegetables. The trees we passed had their trunks painted white from the ground up to a few feet, which made it seem as if we were driving down a street lined with pillars.

As soon as we got out of the taxi, I was hit by a strong smell of hot cooking oil, exhaust, and rotting garbage. I started across the sidewalk, but Lily yanked me back by my shirt.

"You have to be careful here. This is not America. The drivers don't watch out for boys on the street," she said as she handed me the suitcases and carry-ons.

"But I thought this was a sidewalk," I said over the noise of honking.

"Sidewalks or streets – motorbikes and scooters go wherever there's room, so watch out."

As if it had been scripted, a row of motorcycles drove up onto the sidewalk and passed in front of us. One of the drivers had a cloth over his mouth and so did a few of the passengers. It was creepy.

"What are they wearing?" I asked.

"Masks, for the pollution."

"What about helmets?" Dad asked.

"There are no laws for helmets yet. Now follow me. Devon, bring the bags and look out or you'll get hit," she said as she led Dad by the arm across the sidewalk and down a narrow alley. I scrambled behind her and wondered what sort of country didn't watch out for kids on the street and how many kids got killed each day.

She stopped at a door and let herself in. Dad climbed the long set of stairs slowly and I followed.

The family apartment had only three small rooms and a tiny porch that overlooked the street.

"Where're your parents?" Dad asked when we realized nobody was home.

"They must be shopping," Lily said. "And Uncle Tho will be downstairs. I'll go get him soon. But first you need to lie down."

She put Dad to bed in a small back room that overlooked the alley. In it there was enough space for a single bed and a plastic lawn chair.

"Where will *you* sleep?" Dad asked Lily as he laid down.

"In the front room with my parents and Uncle Tho."

"And Devon?"

"There's a spare room downstairs for him."

Sidelined again.

I went to the porch so I could let Lily fuss over Dad for a few minutes. It was crowded with potted plants and the railing was hung with laundry. I stood and watched the chaos below: motorbikes moving in all directions at once; street vendors spilling out over the sidewalk selling everything from lottery tickets to underwear to fish; makeshift food stalls set up with huge pots and customers squatting to eat on brightly painted stools. Pedestrians filled the leftover spaces. As far as I could see down the street there were apartments like the one I was standing in, stacked like a child's building blocks, one on top of another, with tall apartment buildings in the distance. Above the streets, wires stretched like spaghetti noodles across the sky. It was even more intense in real life than it had been on YouTube.

When I went back inside I looked around, but it only took a minute and I'd seen the entire place: two bedrooms and the living room, which was in the middle of the apartment. The living room was accurately named. From what I could see, it was used for everything but sleeping – cooking, eating, sitting, washing. It was hard for me to imagine Quan and Sang living there. I tried to picture them doing their homework at the small plastic table, doing dishes at the basin, but it was impossible to imagine.

The apartment didn't look as if any boys had ever been there.

CHAPTER 15

When Lily took me down to meet Uncle Tho my heart dropped. I tried not to let the shock show on my face, but Uncle Tho didn't look like any doctor I'd ever met. He wasn't wearing hospital clothes or a doctor's coat. He was wearing a long-sleeved shirt and a pair of frayed khakis that were cinched tight with a leather belt.

I waved quickly when Lily introduced us, but he just looked past me and talked to Lily. His office wasn't like any doctor's office I'd ever seen either. There was no waiting room with magazines or toys. There were no nurses or receptionists. There were no stainless steel instruments or bright lights. The room was dim and stacked with jars of dried leaves and powders. There were long thin needles on a counter and a single hard table in the middle of the room. When I looked around that office, my hopes crashed down around me and I doubted Uncle Tho would ever be able to cure Dad. I rubbed my hands against my shorts, hoping I was wrong.

Once Dad was settled and we'd met Uncle Tho, Lily took me to a tiny storage room off the doctor's office. It was full of dusty boxes, but she managed to put a single mat on the floor along with a flat pillow and a bed sheet.

"This is the spare room?" I asked skeptically.

"It's usually the storage room. But now it's the spare room."

"You expect me to sleep down here ... by myself?"

"Where else would you like to sleep?"

"I dunno. Upstairs?"

"Five is enough up there. At least down here you'll have some privacy."

I looked around. The walls were bare, but it wasn't as hot as upstairs, and there was one small window that let in a few rays of light. I yawned and

64

tried to remember what time it was in Vietnam. I was too tired to argue, and besides, I knew there really was no other place to sleep. There was no space in Dad's room, except for under his bed. I wasn't about to sleep in the room with Lily, her parents, and Uncle Tho. So I dropped my bags and followed her back up the stairs.

Even though it was hot and muggy, Lily insisted Dad drink a cup of steaming tea. Then she fussed when he didn't drink enough.

"It is very hot here, which means you need lots of liquids. You'll sweat a lot, so you have to drink a lot."

I watched suspiciously as he sipped from the cup. But I didn't say anything. Instead, I collapsed in the chair in the corner and felt as though I was going to melt. There was one ceiling fan that moved the air slowly, but the room was still suffocating and everything smelled of the fish stall on the street out front. I had only been in the country a few hours and already I wanted to go home.

That first day I sat beside Dad's bed and watched his face. Somehow he slept through the constant sounds from the street below: motorbikes beeping; noodle sellers beating the bottom of their metal woks to attract customers; engines clanking and spluttering; dogs barking, and people yelling. Dad didn't even flinch when a car backfired right outside the window. I'd never heard so much noise. It never let up. What's worse, as darkness fell the noise increased. I didn't think I'd ever be able to sleep the way Dad slept, but somehow, when I finally stumbled downstairs to my mat, everything went pitch black.

* * *

I woke early the next day and went right upstairs to see Dad. He was awake, but he was lying down, sweating in the heat. He smiled when he saw me.

"Hey, how's your room?"

"Good," I lied. "It's a lot cooler down there."

"Did you sleep okay?"

I nodded, then asked, "Have you had anything to drink yet? Do you want me to get you a glass of water?"

"I've had a cup of tea and Lily's gone to the market to get something for breakfast."

I stood in the corner of his room, looked out the window, and described the view to him. He promised to get up and have a look after breakfast.

Uncle Tho came in to see Dad before he went to open his office for the day. Dad smiled and tried to sit up, but Uncle Tho made him lie flat. He looked Dad over carefully, lifting Dad's shirt and shorts. He tested each joint, listened and pressed, tapped and touched every inch of Dad's sick body. Uncle Tho didn't speak while he worked, and he nodded at me only once before he left the room. Then he didn't return again until late in the afternoon, as a heavy rain splashed down outside making the air heavy with moisture. He brought the long thin needles I'd seen in his office and slipped them into Dad's skin with a flick of his wrist. Dad didn't once flinch, but he started to look like a porcupine.

"What are those, anyway?" I dared to ask.

"Acupuncture needles," Dad said.

"Does it hurt?"

"No, actually. I thought it would, but it's okay."

I spent a lot of time watching Uncle Tho work on Dad. Besides acupuncture, Uncle Tho gave Dad massages. He ran his thumb along Dad's spine, pressing down so hard that bruises appeared on his yellow skin. I never spoke to Uncle Tho or Lily or her parents. I just sat in the corner in the unbearable heat and ate whatever was put in front of me. I tried to be invisible in case they noticed me and wanted to send me down to my room so Dad could have some space. Mostly I spoke only to Dad when he woke up.

"Can I get you something?" I asked hopefully when his eyelids fluttered.

"I'm okay, Devon. Thanks for being here," he said and fell back to a motionless sleep.

But as the days wore on, Dad woke less and spoke less. Despite the special foods Lily prepared and the special teas Uncle Tho brewed, Dad got worse. I gave him sponge baths during the hottest part of the day and used a bamboo fan to keep flies off his face. As he got weaker, the panic inside me got stronger, and every time I blinked I was afraid of tears spilling out.

"Are you still here?" Dad asked me once when he opened his eyes, looking unusually alert. It was right after one of Uncle Tho's acupuncture treatments, and for the first time in weeks, I felt hopeful. It was the only sign of strength I'd seen since our arrival.

"Sure. I've been here the whole time," I said.

I kneeled down and held his hand. It felt thin and old. He'd lost a lot of weight since we arrived.

"Shouldn't you be in school?" he asked.

I was confused, so I picked up my books to show him.

"I'm doing my work while you sleep. See? I've already finished my math. I'm going to start on my book report next. When it's done I'll get Lily to take me to an Internet café so I can type it out and send it home."

"You're a good kid, Devon. I'll have to call your mom to tell her what a good kid you are."

"My mom's dead, Dad. You know that, you told me yourself," I said.

I thought maybe the fever had scrambled his brains.

"Nonsense. She lives in the east end of the city. Out by the zoo. On that street with the tire shop. McIntyre. That's where you get that head of hair from."

"McIntyre? That's my mother's last name?"

"Sheila McIntyre. What a ball of energy."

The next time he woke up I tried to ask him more about my mother – about Sheila McIntyre – but all I could get him to say before he fell asleep was, "Whatever happened to Sheila? Haven't seen her in years."

CHAPTER 16

Dad started to vomit blood at the end of our fourth week there. Lily brought a bucket of soapy water and rags and helped me wash him and the floor. She took the dirty sheets and brought clean ones. Then she held Dad's head while he sipped warm tea because he was too weak to sit up. I couldn't tell if Dad was conscious, but he swallowed and kept the tea down for a few hours.

For the first time since we arrived, Uncle Tho didn't come in to work on Dad, and as the day wore on I got more and more upset. In the evening when Lily came into the room with a bowl of rice and vegetables for me to eat, I exploded.

"Where's Uncle Tho? He hasn't been here all day."

"Uncle Tho has a business to run so we can all eat. He can't spend the whole day in here," she said defensively.

"But Dad needs him. Look at him! I think he's getting worse," I pleaded.

"Uncle Tho will come tomorrow. He had to go out today and see patients who couldn't come to him. Besides, your dad needs his rest."

Her tone changed and she spoke more kindly to me than she had in months. But it didn't make me feel better at all.

The next day Dad woke only once. His yellow skin was so shrunken around his skull, he looked like a skeleton.

"I feel so cold," he whispered and then coughed up a wad of phlegm and blood.

I wiped his face with a clean cloth and tried not to cry. "You need to drink more. Here. Lily just brought this tea for you," I lied.

Lily had come in only twice that morning. Once to deliver food to me, and once to bring Dad the hot cup of tea that was now cold.

I propped up his head the way I'd seen Lily do it and put the cup to his lips. He tried to swallow, but the effort was too much for him. I felt tears rolling down my cheek, but I didn't have a free hand to wipe them away.

"Don't cry," he said softly, and I had to sit very still to hear his words.

"I'm not. I just have something in my eye," I said.

I laid his head on the pillow and wiped my eyes with my hands quickly so he wouldn't see I really was crying.

"Don't worry. I'm going to be fine. The main thing is I love you."

I swallowed hard. "I love you too."

"I'm sorry, so sorry," he said before he drifted back to sleep.

When Lily came in that evening I was crying. There was no way to hold it in, and as much as I hated her to see me that way, I couldn't help myself.

"Why are you crying?"

"I know you think I'm stupid, but I'm not. I know Dad's dying," I bawled.

"There's nothing Uncle Tho can do now. Your Dad's *Qi* is too clogged. I think it was already too late when we got here," she said without any emotion, as if only months before she hadn't giggled on the couch with him.

"Aren't you going to do something? Are you just going to let him die?" I sobbed.

"There's nothing I can do."

"We need to get him home so he can get a transplant."

"It's too late, he's too sick to fly now."

"Can't he get a transplant here?"

"I don't think he would even survive the operation."

"I thought you loved him. You're just going to give up?"

"Love has nothing to do with living or dying. Now is his time to die. Before was his time to live and that's when I loved him."

"So now that he's dying you don't love him anymore?"

"There will be nothing left to love soon," she said. Then she glared at me with coal in her eyes. "It's time you go down to your room."

"I want to stay with Dad tonight. I don't want him to be alone."

"It's very late. I'll sit with him. You go to bed."

"I said I don't want to go downstairs. I want to stay with Dad!"

She slapped me across the face with the back of her hand. Her rings split my lip open and I tasted blood on my tongue.

"You don't talk disrespectfully to parents."

"You're not my parent," I said as I held my hand to my face.

"I'm in charge now and I'm telling you to go to your room."

She raised her hand again and I ducked. I took one last look at what was left of my father and ran downstairs to the storage room. I fell on my mat and cried until I heard someone locking the door.

"Hey!" I called out.

There was no answer.

"Uncle Tho?"

There was still no sound. I sat up and shivered. My mind started to spin and my heart raced. I went to the door and tried to open it. I pulled and pounded, but it was locked. I looked up at the window and knew there was no way I could squeeze through it.

I kicked one of the boxes and dented it, then I pounded on the door so hard my hands started to throb. I kicked all of the boxes until the cardboard split open like my lip. But no matter which box I kicked, there were no sounds from outside, and my anger didn't go away. When my feet were too sore to keep kicking I sat down and tried to think of what to do. But there was nothing I *could* do except wait.

CHAPTER 17

I jumped to my feet the next morning when I heard a key in the lock. It was Uncle Tho. He opened the door, then turned and left. I ran upstairs, but Dad's room was empty. I ran to the front room and it was empty too. I ran back downstairs and found Uncle Tho alone in his office.

"Where's my dad?" I said breathlessly.

Uncle Tho stared at me with his saggy yellowed eyes.

"Where did my dad go? Where's Lily?" I asked again, more urgently.

He shook his head and said something in Vietnamese. I was certain he could understand what I was asking, so I stood and stared at him.

"Dead," Uncle Tho said finally as he shuffled slowly around his office, taking jars from the shelves and mixing dried leaves in the palm of his hand.

I stopped breathing, slumped to the floor and buried my head in my arms. The wails that came out of me were so intense I started to choke. I had to lift my head and suck in air like a drowning person. Uncle Tho brought me a cup of tea, but I was shaking so badly I couldn't hold onto anything.

"What is this?" I stuttered between sobs.

"Tea. Drink. Rest."

I shook my head. "You want to poison *me* too?" I spat the words, then wiped my nose with the bottom of my T-shirt.

"Be calm," he said and crouched down to place the cup to my lips.

I was so sick of tea that I wanted to hit the cup out of his hand. But when I looked up at his eyes there was a hint of sadness that surprised me. I sniffed the tea. It smelled different than the teas Lily made for Dad. It smelled musty and I took a careful sip. Despite the odd taste it felt strangely soothing.

"What has she done with him?" I asked quietly, then took another sip.

"Fire," Uncle Tho said and put his free hand on my head, fluffed my hair, and stared at it.

I took a longer sip and my shaking slowed down. I wasn't sure if he was saying that my hair looked like fire or they had taken my dad to be cremated.

"But I wanted to say goodbye," I said slowly. "I wanted to see him one last time."

Then, for some reason, the words I wanted to say slipped out of my reach. I tried again, but I couldn't speak. I tried to take the last sip of tea, but I couldn't move my lips either. Instead I closed my eyes and rested my head on the wall behind me. After that I had a distant sense of someone leading me to my sleeping mat. Before my world went blank, I remembered that it was my birthday – that I'd turned thirteen without anyone noticing.

When I woke up I knew it was evening because I could see the sky had darkened and the sounds of traffic coming from the street were louder. I sat up and felt dizzy, then I laid back down because I was afraid I'd fall. When I tried to recognize where I was, I remembered my father was dead. I started to cry again. I cried until I was out of tears, and then I got up to pee. I stumbled to the door, but it was locked.

"Lily? Uncle Tho? I have to pee. Can you let me out?" I knocked and yelled.

My bladder felt as if it was going to explode, and I fought back fresh tears so I could keep shouting. Finally I heard the key in the door. Again it was Uncle Tho and I ran past him to the toilet.

When I went upstairs, I found Lily's parents eating bowls of soup. They motioned for me to sit down at a fourth bowl, so I did. I hadn't eaten since the previous day and even though I didn't want to eat, my stomach growled loudly. From where I sat, I could see Dad's bedsheets had been changed. Lily was still gone.

"Where's Lily?" I asked.

They shrugged their shoulders. I couldn't tell if they didn't know where Lily was or they didn't understand what I was saying. But before I could figure it out, Uncle Tho appeared with another cup of tea that tasted of the same musty flavor. I drank it and went back down to my room to sleep.

Lily was standing above me and prodding me with her toe when I woke the next time. I opened my eyes, remembered Dad, and felt the tears hit me like a tidal wave. It was as if the drugged sleep made me forget and I had to re-live the horror each time I woke up.

"Come with me," she said.

I stumbled behind her to a taxi waiting outside in the alley. We drove to another busy street in another part of the city and stopped in front of a red door. I didn't realize it was a restaurant until we went inside and sat down. The room was packed with tables and bodies. It smelled of hot oil and fried fish. Men sat eating with chop sticks, and young girls bustled in and out of the kitchen with bowls and plates of food.

"What do you want to eat?" Lily asked me.

What I wanted more than anything was spaghetti and meatballs, but instead I ordered lemongrass beef with rice noodles. It was the closest thing.

"Where's Dad?" I asked finally when I realized she wasn't going to tell me.

"Cremated. His ashes are here."

She took a small wooden box out of her bag and handed it to me. I took it in my hands. She hadn't even asked me what to do with my own father's body. I wiped tears off my cheeks.

"You cry a lot for a boy," she said.

Her comment winded me, but I didn't react. I knew she was just trying to make me angry.

Shortly after we ordered, an older lady came to our table and stared at me. She had graying hair and stern eyes. When she looked me up and down, I felt a shiver over my whole back. She stepped close and started to play with my hair, but I swatted her hand away. I didn't know who she was, but I wanted her to go away. I wanted to talk to Lily in private. I needed to find out when we were leaving because more than anything I ached to get home and away from her and this nightmare. But the lady didn't appear to be in any hurry to leave. In fact, she sat down across from Lily and they started to talk in quick, short sentences. At first they were polite to one another, and even though I didn't know what was being said, I knew Lily well enough to know she was making a deal. Soon their voices rose, and, at one point, the lady stood up to leave. But then Lily nodded and shortly after the lady left. Lily looked relieved.

"When are we going home?" I asked when we were finally alone.

"Next week," Lily said.

"Why so long?"

"It was the first flight I could get and there's paperwork. You can't just fly home with someone's ashes without doing the paperwork."

"I want to call home."

"You know we don't have a phone at the apartment."

"I'll use a pay phone."

"It's very expensive. Besides, it's too hard with the time difference."

"Can you take me to a computer then? I want to send an email. I want to tell my teachers what's going on. They'll be expecting my assignments. And I want to email Vic. Isn't there a number he can call me at?"

"Maybe tomorrow. Today I have a lot to do."

She sat tall and stared straight ahead without saying another word. Even on the taxi ride home she didn't speak or look at me.

In the apartment, when Lily went back out, Uncle Tho gave me another cup of his tea.

"What is this, anyway? Is too much of it bad for me?"

He shook his head. "Drink. Rest."

I was too confused and worn out to argue, so I drank it and let myself escape into a deep sleep again.

CHAPTER 18

The next time I woke up I was lying on a cot in a windowless room. There was no other furniture and the walls were dirty. I could hear voices through the door – voices that I didn't recognize. And the smell from the fish stand that filled Lily's family apartment was replaced now with the smell of cigarette smoke. When I saw my backpack by the door, the first thing I thought was that we were going home – that Lily had packed to get us ready for our trip and somehow I'd been moved in my sleep. I wondered if I'd slept away a whole week, but I didn't care – I just wanted to get on a plane and away from Vietnam. I didn't think past getting home, back to my city and friends, back to people who cared about me. Even though I knew I wouldn't have my father there – ever again – and that I'd never be able to stand living with Lily, I couldn't wait to leave.

When the door opened, I jumped up expecting to see Lily. Instead I saw the older lady from the restaurant who had played with my hair. She was wearing glasses this time, and her hair was pulled back tightly.

"Lại đây!" she said and pointed to my backpack.

I looked at my backpack and then at her.

"Lại đây!" she said and pointed at my backpack again, only this time she sounded more aggravated.

"Lại đây! Come," she said sternly. She stepped toward me, grabbed my shirt and tugged.

I picked up my backpack and followed her out to the sidewalk and into a waiting taxi.

"Where's Lily?" I asked as I got in.

"Gone," the lady said in a thick accent.

"Gone where?" I asked.

"Home."

"Home where?"

"America."

"She left without me?"

Questions swirled in my head. Did Lily get an earlier flight? Who was this lady? Why was I going with her? Why didn't Lily tell me I was going home by myself? Where was my ticket and passport? I finally managed to ask, "Are we going to the airport now?"

The lady shook her head.

"Where are we going?"

She waved her hands and spoke quickly in Vietnamese, then in English she said: "Wait and see."

"But I just want to know where we're going," I said.

She turned her head away and I stopped trying to talk. I looked out the window instead. Although I hadn't been out of the apartment much since we arrived, the streets looked different and the air was different too – it was still humid and smelled of rotting plants, but the exhaust fumes were stronger. There were fewer motorbikes, but there were more bicycles and people walking. The buildings were more run down and, when we passed by the odd tree, I noticed the trees were smaller and the trunks weren't painted white as they had been near Lily's neighborhood. I felt as if I was in a completely different part of the city.

We turned down a narrow street and pulled up in front of a plain two-story block building. There was a hand-painted sign on the wall, but I couldn't read what it said. The street was busy with bicycles and with people walking by. I could tell by the sun that it was morning, that people were on their way to work. Another taxi honked to get past us, but there wasn't enough room for two cars.

"Come," the lady said.

She got out of the taxi and paid the fare. I stood close to the wall while she unlocked the door. Then she waited while I stepped inside ahead of her. There were no lights on, so it took my eyes a second to adjust and see that we were inside another restaurant.

"Come," she said again and led me through the kitchen and down a dark narrow set of stairs. She opened a door to another dimly lit room with four cots. The ceiling was low – just barely above my head. My heart was pounding as hard and fast as a baby rabbit's – like the one Vic once found stranded in the park and tried to save.

"What are we doing here? When are we going to the airport?"

"No airport. You work now."

"What do you mean?"

"I buy you. You work for me."

"What? You bought me and I work for you?"

"Yes, I bought you and you work for me now," she repeated.

"But I don't want a job. I just want to go home." The beads of sweat doubled on my forehead. My shoulders shook and my vision blurred.

She took my backpack and shoved me into the room. I fell on the floor against a cot.

"Shoes."

"What?"

"Give me your shoes."

"Why?"

"So you don't run."

She leaned down and yanked them off my feet. I tried to fight back, but she kicked me hard in the side.

"You're mine. Very expensive. But I will make it back. *Tóc hung hung đỏ*. Everyone loves fire hair," she said and stepped away with my things.

"My backpack!" I screamed and reached out.

"Be good and get it later," she said and slammed the door.

As soon as I realized she was locking me in, I rushed forward and tried to push the door open. I screamed and banged.

"You can't keep me here. You can't just buy people. Someone will come looking for me and you'll be in trouble. Let me out! This is a mistake! Let me out of here. Hey! Someone?"

I yelled and yelled, but nobody came. When I stopped to catch my breath, I heard a radio from above, then footsteps and running water. I looked around quickly and again noticed the four cots, clothes hanging on hooks, a small open window near the top of one wall that let in a stray beam of light and the smell of rotting meat. I sat down on one of the cots and put my head in my hands.

When I felt a cool palm on the back of my neck a moment later, I jumped up and screamed. A boy my age jumped away from me.

"Sorry! I thought I was alone. Are you locked in too?" I asked.

He spoke so fast I couldn't understand anything he was saying.

"Did that lady buy you too?" I asked slowly and sat down again.

He nodded.

"Why are we here? What's going on?"

He didn't answer. He only watched me wipe my eyes and peer into the dark corners of the room. As my eyes cleared, I saw there were two other boys. They came slowly out of the shadows and sat down on the cot with me. They stroked my hair and spoke to one another in low whispers. I raised my hand and they scattered to the corner. I was so tired of people touching my hair that I started sobbing.

I had no idea what was going on, but I knew I was in more danger than I'd ever imagined possible.

Part 2: Long

CHAPTER 19

I don't know how long I cried, but eventually I curled into a ball and fell asleep. When I awoke there was a skinny band of light hitting my cheek and I was still in a half-dream where Dad was cheering for me at a baseball game. He was yelling, "Go, Devon! You can do it. Go!"

When I remembered the dream and felt the sunbeam, I sat up. I rubbed my eyes and promised myself I'd clear my mind and find a way to get my things and get away as soon as possible. I got up and explored the small room while the boys watched. I examined every inch of each of the four walls, then stood on my tiptoes to look out the window. The walls were solid concrete. The window was open to the outside, but it was too narrow and it was protected by bars: I could only get my hands out. I stood with my head near the ceiling to see what was outside. There were garbage bins and bicycles. There was a wall of a nearby building and a cement trench directly in front, running with water from a recent rainfall. The sounds and smells of the city rushed in, and the stench of hot rotting garbage and urine made me gag. When I finished looking out the window, I went to the door and threw my shoulder against it. It was shut tight and it didn't take long to realize I'd never escape that room. I'd have to find another way out.

I turned and for the first time approached the boys. I thought they were just sitting on the cement floor, but as I got closer I saw they were playing a game with dice. The dice were hand-carved. As the tallest boy threw them, they all began to chatter.

"I'm Devon," I said.

They stood together to face me.

"Devon," I said again, patting myself on the chest.

"I'm Minh," said the tallest boy, patting himself. Then he pointed to the other two boys and said: "This is An and Hien."

I repeated each of the boys' names and they nodded. Then we took turns repeating "Devon" over and over until they could say it.

"You speak English?" I asked hopefully.

"A little," Minh said.

"What are we doing here?"

"We work here," he said as he examined his fingernails.

"Upstairs? In the restaurant?"

He nodded and looked back up at me.

"Are we always locked in?"

He nodded again, slowly.

"Is there a way out?"

"No. Just work to pay your debt."

"What debt?" I asked. I couldn't understand how I could owe anyone any money.

"The cost to buy you and feed you while you are here."

"How much do I owe?" I said, thinking of my bank account back home that had a few hundred dollars worth of birthday money in it.

He shrugged. "They keep track. When it is all paid, they let you go."

"Will I get my things back?"

He shrugged.

"But I really need my things. It's everything I have with me here – my clothes and my schoolbooks, my money. She even took my shoes."

He looked down at his feet and when I followed his gaze, I noticed his feet were bare too. I didn't say it out loud, but what I really wanted were the pictures of me and Dad that were tucked in the back of my wallet.

"How long have you been here?" I asked quietly.

He shrugged. "Two years, maybe longer."

It felt as if someone had kicked me in the stomach. I sank back onto a cot to catch my breath.

"And the others?" I asked finally. "How long have they been here?"

"An was here when I came. Hien came after."

"How did you end up here?"

The question made him shudder. "That is a long story. Maybe best for another day," he said finally.

"How did you learn English?"

"I studied in school ... before I came here. When tourists come, I learn more."

"Do the others speak English?" I asked as I nodded toward An and Hien. The two of them stared back.

"No, just me," Minh confirmed.

Just then I heard a key in the door. I jumped up with the others and stepped back into the corner. The same lady appeared with four bowls, four small cups, and a cracked teapot. She ducked inside and left everything on a tray on the ground, then she locked the door behind her again.

"Who's she?" I asked, pointing at the door after she left.

"Long," Minh said. "She is the boss. Always do what she says. Always". Then he reached for his bowl and gulped down his food like a hungry dog.

I suddenly realized how hungry I was, so I grabbed my bowl too. It was filled with plain rice and a few bits of vegetable. The tea was mostly just hot water, but Minh poured it equally in each cup. It took me only a minute to finish my share, and when I was done, I wished there was more.

When the door opened again, the boys lined up and Long watched them file past her. I followed, but when I got to the door she spoke sharply.

"You stay," she said and knocked me backward with her fist.

Blood poured down my chin and my eyes watered. It felt as if my nose had been crushed, and as I crawled back to my cot, I used one hand to stop the bleeding. I didn't dare look up, but I heard the key in the lock again. That's when the room closed in on me and I realized just how low the ceiling was and how close the walls were on each side. I mopped the blood from my face with the bottom of my T-shirt and promised not to cry, no matter how much blood poured from me. I knew I couldn't think about being scared and instead had to focus on escaping. I didn't yet know how I would get out, but I knew I had to find a way.

CHAPTER 20

When the boys returned, Minh came directly to me and held my face to the light bulb that dangled from the ceiling. He examined my nose and the blood on my shirt. Then he went to the row of hooks and sorted through the clothes until he found me a clean T-shirt. It was a Yankees shirt and I was happy to trade it for my bloodied one. An and Hien lay on their cots and I sat down on mine. Minh sat beside me.

"Are you hungry?" he asked and pulled a small paper package from his pocket.

I unfolded it and found a few hunks of cold meat.

"This is for me?" I asked.

"Yes, we ate upstairs," he said.

I tipped the package into my mouth and swallowed so quickly I almost choked. It wasn't much, but it helped fill the empty feeling in my stomach.

The next time the door opened Long dropped a bucket inside, spoke quickly, and wagged her finger at us. She glared at me, then slammed the door.

"If you have to go, use the bucket," Minh said, then laid down on his cot.

I stared long and hard at the bucket. I couldn't believe we were supposed to pee in it, that we weren't even allowed to use a toilet. I really had to go, but I didn't want the others to watch. As if they could read my mind, the three of them rolled over to face the wall. I hesitated, but the burning in my bladder helped me make up my mind.

When I finished, Minh put the bucket in the corner of the room and covered it with a square of cardboard.

"We always cover it. To keep the smell inside," he said.

Then he laid back down on his cot and I laid on mine.

I listened as the sounds from upstairs gradually faded. When the kitchen was completely quiet, Minh said, "The restaurant is closed now."

"Does everyone go home? Are we alone?" I asked.

Minh nodded. "They come back in the morning."

I jumped up and stood on my tiptoes. I jammed my head against the ceiling so I could look out the window. Sure enough the bicycles were gone and the garbage bins were closed. I realized I had a chance to yell for help, without Long hearing. I'd yell until someone heard me this time – all night if I had too.

"Help! Somebody! They've got us trapped down here. Somebody. Help!" I screamed as loud as I could, but the others pulled me away from the window and Minh scolded me.

"What's wrong?" I asked. "Someone will hear us. They can get the police."

"No! Long will hear you. She is waiting. To see if you stay quiet."

The boys stared at me. I could see the tension in their shoulders. Then the light bulb went out.

"That's all? She turns out the light when we do something wrong?" I almost felt like laughing, but the others looked frightened.

"No. She beats us too. But you are different, I think. She is nicer to you."

"You call that nice? The way she treats me?"

"Yes. Your red hair. It makes you special."

I didn't ask any more questions, but I thought hard about why I was treated differently from the other boys. I felt suddenly close to them – to Minh especially – and I knew that when I got free, I'd find a way to help them too.

When the last rays of daylight faded completely, the room slipped into blackness. It was so dark I couldn't even see the shapes of the cots or the boys lying on them. I heard Hien whimper in the corner and I realized suddenly that the night was going to be long. I remembered waking up in the dark as a little kid and calling out for Dad, how he came and turned on the bedside lamp. Even though I wasn't afraid of monsters under my bed anymore, I knew the light would have made us all feel safer and that it was my fault we were sitting in the dark. If only I had my backpack, I thought, we'd have a flashlight.

Instead, to fill the void, I surprised myself. I sat up and started to sing. I began quietly, then I let my voice fill the room. I didn't have a good voice, but the others didn't seem to mind. I sang all of my favorite songs and all of Vic's. Then I started singing some of the old songs Dad used to play on our CD player before Lily moved in. When I stopped singing, the boys clapped their hands until I sang again. I sang for hours. I sang every song I'd ever known and I even made up extra stanzas. I sang until my throat was too dry to continue. Then I lay in the dark and tried to remember as much as I could about the taxi ride with Long so I'd have a clue about where I was. I forced myself to remember as many details as I could and listened to the sounds of the city as it settled in for the night. Beyond the street noises I could hear someone coughing above me, and before I fell asleep, I wondered who could be so close and if there were more kids like us, hidden away in other rooms.

CHAPTER 21

The first thing I saw when I opened my eyes the next morning was An peeing into the bucket. The other two boys were watching me from their cots, so I rolled over and concentrated on not crying. My stomach ached, both from being hungry and from remembering where I was. I wished I never had to get up. But when the key rattled in the door, I jumped into line like a soldier. Long dropped our tray of food on the floor. She spoke sharply, and Minh nodded without looking up.

"Take that," she said to me and pointed to the bucket. "And don't run."

I carried the bucket carefully up the stairs behind Minh and tried not to breathe in the smell. He led me to a small washroom at the back of the restaurant and waited while I went inside.

"Can I use the toilet?" I asked hopefully.

"No. Just empty the bucket," he said.

I poured the pee down the toilet and flushed.

"Rinse and fill it with water."

I followed his instructions and resisted the urge to stop and wash my hands.

"Now come quickly!" he said.

He picked up a wash basin and a bar of soap and rushed back down the stairs ahead of me. I scrambled to keep up, wondering what the hurry was. But then I saw Long waiting by the door with her arms crossed. Minh hesitated then ducked past her. I followed as quickly as I could, but she kicked me when I went by.

"You wash clothes today," she said to me as I crouched on the floor and scooped rice into my mouth.

I nodded and swallowed. My leg throbbed, but I went and picked a shirt from one of the hooks and started to scrub.

"Do a good job," Long barked, then she led the boys upstairs.

I washed everything in the room, even my bloody shirt, then I stretched them out on the hooks to dry. When I finished the last ragged bedsheet, Minh appeared with a bucket of clean water and a bag of dirty cloths from the restaurant. I scrubbed until my arms felt like rubber and the skin on my fingers were wrinkled like raisins. Just when I'd neared the end of one batch of dirty laundry, Minh would appear with another: towels, washcloths, rags, sheets, pillowcases. After the linens there were more clothes: skirts, blouses, t-shirts, dresses, pants. I had no idea where all the dirty laundry could be coming from, but I washed with as much energy as I could, hoping that I'd somehow please Long enough that she'd let me join the others upstairs. Then, I hoped, I'd have a better chance of figuring out how I could get out.

I washed laundry all that week and the following week. Then one morning, when I'd lost track of how many days I'd been washing, Long motioned for me to follow the other boys.

"*Lại đây!*" she said.

I lined up timidly and followed the others upstairs, but instead of going into the restaurant, I was sent into the kitchen. It was cramped and hot in there and everything was coated in oil – even the floor felt slippery under my bare feet. There were no windows and there was only one way out – past the cook who whacked me across the back of the head with a heavy wooden spoon when I walked by. Long led me to the sink where a stack of dirty dishes towered nearby.

"Scrape. Wash. Then leave them to dry," she said roughly as she pointed to the garbage bin, the sink, and a drying rack.

I started to scrape the dirty bowls while Long filled the sink with hot water and bleach. She spilled the bowls into the sink then looked at me, waiting for me to begin washing. There was steam rising from the water and the bleach was so strong it stung my nose. I stepped back. But she grabbed my arm and quickly pulled me forward. I had no choice, so I plunged my hands into the sink, then yelled and pulled them out. She slapped me hard across the head and I reached back into the scalding water. My eyes stung with tears and my skin burned, but I kept my head down.

"Hot water cleans better," she said.

For the first couple of hours I scraped the dishes into the garbage bin. Then I couldn't stand it any longer. When I saw a pork dumpling, my body took over. I reached out and popped it into my mouth. I braced for the cook to whack me again, but he must not have noticed. After that I got braver and whenever I saw a good scrap of food, as quick as the flicker of a snake's tongue, I slipped it into my mouth. That day I ate half a boiled egg, several bites of fish, and some stewed chicken. For the first time in weeks my stomach didn't hurt. By the end of the day I'd also tucked a spring roll and a rice patty into my pocket. Somehow the act of stealing raised my spirits and reminded me I'd find a way out. What lay beyond the restaurant, I barely knew: strangers, streets, and chaos. But I was sure if I could get out and run, I'd find someone to help me.

From where I worked in the kitchen, I could see only a block wall and I was afraid to look around. I wanted to look up when I heard the boys come in for plates of food, but I didn't dare turn around. Instead, I tried to recognize the sound of their steps.

When I heard the cook leave the kitchen one afternoon, after a few days of washing dishes, I didn't wait. I ran into the restaurant where two men glanced up from their plates, then over at Long who was standing by the door. I saw that I'd never get past her and I froze. But before I could get back to the kitchen, she rushed forward and slapped me hard across the face. Stars flew in my eyes and I had to blink to clear them. I looked to see if any of the customers saw what happened and if they would help me, but everyone just kept eating. Long grabbed me by the arm and dragged me back to the sink.

"You want to work out front?" she spat.

I nodded numbly.

"Good. You start tomorrow."

That night, when I told Minh I was getting a new job, he looked worried and told me it was better to wash dishes than work out front. I hadn't told him my plan to escape, so I didn't expect him to understand. But his reaction bothered me.

The next afternoon, Long put An on dishes and took me into the restaurant. It was cramped with plastic tables and mismatched chairs, and the sound of so many people talking made the place seem even more crowded. The dingy yellow walls were plastered with posters of smiling women. I wrinkled my nose at the smell of sweaty bodies and I wished the ceiling fans actually moved the air. I looked for a way out and saw the door was closed tight and the one small window in the room was covered by mesh wire, so I could barely even see what was outside.

Minh was running from table to table, delivering food and clearing dishes. He was sweating like crazy in the heat while men ate and wiped their foreheads. But Hien was nowhere to be found. When one of the men stood up and nodded to Long, she whistled. Minh quickly dropped an armload of dirty dishes then headed to the back of the restaurant. The man followed. I craned my neck to see where they were going, but Long elbowed me in the ribs. Then she handed me a plastic bin.

"Clear all the dirty dishes. Hien will be back soon."

Since I was the only one left working, I had to scramble to catch up and I didn't notice when Hien reappeared. He was suddenly carrying plates of food and running back to the kitchen for more.

It soon became clear that only Minh was allowed to take meal orders. When he was out of the room, Long left her chair by the front door where she greeted the men coming in and took the orders to the cook. I watched closely then to see if I had enough time to run, but Long was never gone for more than a few seconds – just long enough to poke her head into the kitchen and bark at the cook. Then she marched right back to the door. Even though I was fast, I knew I'd need a twenty-second head-start to get outside and down the street far enough so I wouldn't get caught again. But when I counted in my head, I never got past seven "Mississippis."

That evening, after we'd emptied our pockets and shared what food we had, I noticed Minh was quieter than usual. He curled up on his cot with his back to us.

"Are you okay?" I asked.

I put my arm on his shoulder, but he pulled away without speaking. An and Hien watched but didn't move.

"Are you sick?" I asked, but this time I was careful not to touch him.

When he still didn't answer, I leaned over and saw his cheeks were wet with tears.

"What's the matter?" I asked, then remembered the man he left the restaurant with.

"Did something happen with that man? Did he hurt you?" I asked and felt my stomach suddenly ache more than usual.

An and Hien kept their heads down and held tightly onto the dice.

"Minh, where did you go this afternoon with that man?" I asked again.

Finally, without moving, Minh said, "You will find out soon."

A terrifying thought flashed across my mind, but I tried to keep it from forming too clearly. I didn't want to think about what other work Minh was forced to do for Long's customers. I looked quickly at An, then at Hien, and even though they couldn't speak English, the looks of shame on their faces scared me. My lungs tightened and I struggled to breathe.

That's when I knew Long didn't run a regular restaurant.

CHAPTER 22

"That man ... he made you do things with him, didn't he?" I asked finally, when I caught my breath.

Minh still didn't answer, but he rolled over slowly and the look on his face told me I was right. I felt my last meal wash up the back of my throat. I struggled to understand what was happening to me, I tried to understand how I went from being a regular everyday American kid to being trapped in a basement in Vietnam.

"Do An and Hien go with him?" I asked, afraid to ask the real question – if *I* would have to go with him one day too.

Finally Minh spoke.

"No, that one always asks for me. I hate him. I hate them all. But him the most."

The emotion in Minh's voice made me shiver, and I wrapped a bed sheet tight around my shoulders.

"Do all the men come for the same thing?" I asked, hoping that most came for the food.

"No, some come for the girls."

"The girls?"

"Yes, Long keeps girls upstairs."

"How many?"

"Five or six."

"That's why I hear coughing sometimes in the night?"

Minh nodded. I wasn't surprised – I'd suspected it from the beginning but was afraid to ask.

"How did they get here?"

Minh shrugged. "We all got here different ways."

"How did you get here?"

It took Minh a long time to answer. He didn't look at me. He just played with a loose thread on his shirt as he spoke. He told me about where he lived with his parents and brothers and how he used to walk to the next village to his grandfather's house every day after school. His grandfather was old and sick so Minh's mother sent food for him. It wasn't far but the road was usually deserted. One day two men came in a car and grabbed Minh. He struggled to get free, but they were too strong. They tied his arms and legs and covered his mouth with tape. They put him in the trunk of the car and moved him from place to place over many days. Then they sold him to Long. Minh said the first months were the worst and he cried every day. But one of the boys told Minh he could work off his debt and go home. He told Minh to hang onto the idea that he would see his family again.

"Where did that boy go?" I asked.

"He worked off his debt and went home," Minh said, but he didn't seem very sure.

"Have you ever tried to get away?" I asked.

"No, but there were others who tried. They were caught and beaten." He hesitated and searched for words before he said, "*Never* try to run away." He shuddered, and I realized he wasn't telling me everything.

"What about An? Did men steal him too?"

Minh shook his head. "His mother sent him after his father died. She could not feed six children. Long is An's cousin. She said he could get work here in Cambodia. So An's mother sent him to work in this restaurant. Long sends money back to his family, but his mother has no idea what An does. She thinks An works nights in the restaurant and goes to school in the day."

"Wait – did you say we're in Cambodia?" I asked, confused.

Minh nodded.

"We're not in Vietnam?"

"No. We were brought here from Vietnam," Minh said. "I was brought over at night. They hid me in the back of a truck. I had to lie for hours in a box no bigger than this cot. It was so hard to breathe. I thought I would die."

Even though I was sitting, I leaned against the wall for balance. I tried to line up my thoughts, but I couldn't even picture where Cambodia was on a map. I knew nothing about Cambodia.

"Are we near Vietnam?"

"In Phnom Penh. Only a few hours from Ho Chi Minh City."

"How did I get here?"

"Probably drugged like Hien. Then hidden in a car."

"Hien was kidnapped too?"

"Yes. Hien says even though they were poor, his mother would never have sold him. She always warned him not to go with strangers who promised good jobs or money."

I looked at Hien and An sitting on the floor with their dice, and my chest tightened. I now understood how scared they were and that they used the dice as a way to forget. I looked back at Minh and we shared a long moment of silence.

"I can't believe I've been in Cambodia," I finally muttered.

"I thought you knew," Minh said quietly.

"What about the girls? Are they Vietnamese or Cambodian?"

"Vietnamese, I think. Long brings us here because it is harder for us to escape. We don't speak the language, and there is no chance of our families finding us."

When Minh and I stopped talking, An rolled the dice and motioned for us to join him. I laid on my cot instead. Apparently a basement in Cambodia was the same as a basement in Vietnam, and since I wasn't allowed to talk to the customers or go outside, I'd never noticed. All I ever did was go from the basement to the restaurant and back. I knew it didn't matter what country I was in. My days were made up of a few small rooms and being in Cambodia or Vietnam didn't make a difference.

Even though Minh believed he'd pay back his debt and be free, I knew it was impossible that Long would ever let me go. I knew there was no debt I could ever repay. She had bought me from Lily and she thought she owned me forever. If she'd ever let any of the other boys or girls go, I was sure she'd have been caught by now. I was sure that when she was through with one of them, she sold them somewhere else. I couldn't let myself think what else she might do.

I thought about the man who took Minh from the restaurant. I was sure Lily knew what Long bought me for and my hate for her spilled into the room.

"I'm going to get out and make her pay for this," I said out loud with as much confidence as I could.

CHAPTER 23

Word must have gotten out that Long had a new boy at her place because the restaurant got busier. Men came in to look at me. They walked right up and played with my hair, looked into my eyes, and examined my freckles. I felt like one of the zoo animals that we used to visit at home, and I knew right then, without a doubt, that those animals wanted to be free.

Then one day Minh overheard the customers talking about an auction Long was holding. He told me there was a "bidding war" going on among the regular customers, the ones who pretended to come in for the food and the girls. These men were bidding for the first chance to be with me, and I knew I had only a few more days before one of them would take me away. I was so scared that I couldn't eat or sleep at all. I got dizzy whenever I stood up, and I started to cough. Minh gave me an extra cup of the hot tea each night to soothe my throat.

"You have to eat and drink. If you get sick, you will never get home," he said one night when the coughing left me exhausted.

"What will I do?" I asked. I was trembling so badly I spilled tea on myself when I took the cup from him.

"Whatever they want."

"But how?"

"Keep your mind blank. Or think about the beating they will give you if you fight. Even if they break all your bones, they won't call a doctor. If you die, they just find another boy."

"Where do they take you?"

"Upstairs."

"There's no way out from upstairs?"

Minh shook his head. "The windows are too high. There is no door."

"What about the girls? Can they help?"

"If they could help, they would not be there."

"But there has to be some way," I muttered and imagined myself, once more, pushing past Long and running free.

I sipped the tea and even in the heat, shivered under my bedsheet. I fought with myself to believe I'd get out of that basement, that Dad was watching over me and would help me find a way. I even let myself think of home. That night I remembered playing X-Box with Vic and Eric and Cody. I remembered Mrs. Lamba wishing me a good trip when she handed me my math assignments. I remembered promising Vic I'd be home for the track meet and realized with a sinking feeling that it was long past. What did they think? And how had Lily explained me not coming back with her? I was sure Vic or Cody would have asked Quan or Sang about me, or would have gone by the house to find out where I was. But I had no idea how long it would take anyone to find me, or if they would even think to look in Cambodia.

* * *

The following morning, it happened.

Long called me over. "A special customer is upstairs waiting. He paid a lot of money. Do what he wants," she said.

I glanced at the front door, but it was closed. When she saw me looking, she pushed me toward the back of the building where the stairs went up. I stumbled but didn't fall.

"First room on the right. Hurry," she said.

I walked slowly. I thought of Minh's warning, but I still looked for an escape. The hallway was narrow and empty with rows of doors on each side. Only one door was open. There was no place to hide and nowhere else to go.

I stepped inside the room. I didn't look at the man sitting on the bed. I just waited with my face to the floor. All I could see were the man's shiny black shoes and pant legs as he stepped over to close the door behind me. Then he sat back down and spoke. I didn't understand what he said and when I didn't move, he reached for me. That's when my body took over and I fought him like a scared cat. I scratched and kicked and yelled until he yanked my arm high up behind my back and put his hand over my mouth. My shoulder screamed with pain and I stopped fighting. He smelled like sweat mixed with cigarette smoke and I started to gag. I didn't mean to, but I bit into his hand until I tasted blood. He shouted and let me go. Then, before I could even duck, he started hitting me with his fists.

"I'm sorry. I'm sorry. Please stop. Please!" I cried and put my arms up to protect myself. But he was so much bigger than me that I didn't stand a chance. Even when I was on the floor crying, he kicked me again and again. By the time he finished, I was crumpled on the floor, gasping for air.

I was afraid Long would come up to beat me more, but the next person I saw was a teenage girl wearing a short red skirt and tank top. Her hair flowed over her shoulders. I was afraid I was dead and that she was a ghost. She brought a rag and a bowl of water and hummed while she patted my face.

"Never fight back. It makes it worse. You are lucky to be alive. You are lucky to have that red hair Long admires so much," she said softly.

I wasn't sure why she was allowed to help me, but I was relieved to be with her. I tried to speak, but my lips were swollen and I must have been slurring because she hushed me and continued to clean me up. She felt my ribcage, I guess for broken ribs. Then she helped me onto the bed and poured cold water into my mouth. I winced and she apologized.

"What is your name?" she asked finally.

"Devon."

"I knew it was not Red. That is what the men call you, you know."

I hated the fact that they called me Red, but the anger disappeared under the pain.

"Where are you from?" she asked gently, and I knew she was trying to distract me.

"America."

"How did you end up here?"

"I was in Vietnam with my father and his girlfriend, Lily. He was sick and Lily said her uncle could cure him. But my dad died and then Lily sold me to Long."

She didn't seem surprised.

"How old are you, anyway?" she asked.

"Thirteen. How old are you?"

"Sixteen."

I squinted up at her. She looked much younger.

"How long have you been here?"

"Five years, I think."

Goosebumps sprung up across my skin. "Have you tried to get out?"

She shook her head. "Long locks us in at night. I tried to yell for help when I first came, but she beat me like this. So I stopped."

"Will you ever get out?"

"I hope so," she said quietly.

"What will happen now?"

"Long will take you back downstairs. When the bruises are gone she will put you back to work. You better not fight next time. The beatings get worse."

I shuddered at the thought. I wanted to roll over and cry, go to sleep, maybe never wake up. Just then I heard Long's footsteps on the stairs.

"What's your name?" I asked quickly.

"Tham."

"Will I see you again?"

"Not like this, I hope," she said and then backed out of the room.

Long barged in and screamed at me. "*Ngu như lừa!* Trying to get yourself killed? *Lại đây!*"

She dragged me by the arm down to our room. It hurt to move, but I swallowed the pain and collapsed on my cot.

"Next time do what you are told. Then you get your things back."

The promise of seeing my things choked me. I'd have done almost anything to see the photos of my dad.

CHAPTER 24

When my bruises faded, I went to clear and wash dishes again. The man who beat me came into the restaurant one day shortly after. Long called me over. She gave me a small cup of tea and sent me upstairs to drink it and wait.

"Don't fight," she warned.

I walked slowly up the stairs again, went into the same small dark room, and sat down on the bed. I sipped the tea and recognized the musty taste from my days with Uncle Tho.

Other than a narrow bed and a white plastic chair the room was empty and the walls were plastered with pages from magazines. There was no window in the room, and I wished there was one I could look out, one that I could put my face next to, even for a few minutes so I could feel a breeze or feel the sun on my face. I hadn't been outside for months. I could hear noises in the rooms around me: shuffling bodies, moans, creaking floor boards. I shivered, but I felt strangely calm. The tea was taking effect.

I heard footsteps outside the door and glanced up with dread, but it was not the man from before. It was a different man scurrying along the hall. I looked at my hands and tried to wish myself away.

"So this is what you look like. When you are not beaten?"

The voice startled me and when I looked up, Tham was standing in the door.

"Tham!" I said.

She saw the tea cup in my hand.

"Long gave you the calming tea?"

I nodded.

"She doesn't trust you. She thinks you will fight again."

"I couldn't help it."

"I know. The tea will help."

I felt dizzy, so I laid on my side with my knees tucked up to my chin.

"He's going to be here soon," I whispered.

"Shhhh," she said and smoothed the hair away from my face the way my father used to do when I had nightmares.

"Try to relax."

I could feel my breathing slow down, and it was hard to keep my eyes open.

"Go ahead and close them," Tham said.

Her voice was slow and far away. I wanted to ask her to stay with me, but I couldn't open my mouth. I fell into blackness.

* * *

When I awoke I was alone, lying on the bed under a thin sheet. It felt as if an hour or two had passed because the sounds from outside had changed and an afternoon rain pounded on the roof. I blinked to clear my vision and I struggled to pull my clothes on. My head ached and my arms trembled. I was afraid I might puke. Then I saw my backpack by the door. The sight of it made my temples pound. I was still dizzy, but I stood up and stepped across the room, using the wall for balance. I grabbed it and stumbled back to the bed and finally managed to open the zipper. Inside were most of my things: my copies of Skateboarder Magazine; my favorite baseball cap; my toiletries; the flashlight; shorts and T-shirts; my school books and notebooks; my wallet, though my identification and money were gone. I held my breath and opened the back flap of the wallet, desperate to find the pictures of me and Dad.

I pulled them out and stared at them – stared at my father's familiar face. The day we took those photos came back to me. It had been during a cold snap in January and we went to the mall just because we'd already watched three back-to-back Star Wars movies. We checked out a new video game at the computer store, then stopped at the food court for lunch. On the way by the photobooth, Dad got all excited and insisted we go in.

"Make your goofiest face," he said as we squeezed beside each other.

"You won't even need to try," I teased.

Then the camera went off and we laughed and tried to get ready for the next picture.

As I sat on the bed, I wiped the tears streaming down my face so I wouldn't ruin the photos and then tucked them carefully back inside my wallet. I was thinking about changing into clean clothes, but Long was suddenly at the door.

"Come," she said.

I held tightly to my backpack and followed her down the hall to a restroom.

"Five minutes," she said and locked me in.

I used my T-shirt and soap to wash. I felt dirtier than I did after a shift at the meat works and I wanted to scrub my skin right off. I wanted to slide out of it the way a snake sheds its old skin. I didn't want any part of me that had been touched by that man to be left on me. But I knew my time was running out so I pulled on clean clothes and put on deodorant. If I hadn't been crying so hard, I might have appreciated the running water and privacy more. Usually we had to all wash together from a bucket in our room.

When Long opened the door again, I was clean and dressed. I shoved everything into my backpack and stood up with my eyes cast down.

"One bad move and I will take it back," she said before she snorted and led me down to our room.

The boys swarmed me when I stepped inside with the backpack.

"Do you want to see?" I asked.

They pulled over a cot and watched as I pulled everything out and laid it beside me. The first thing Minh did was flip through my schoolbooks. An tried on my cap. Hien held up each of my shirts. I grabbed my toiletry bag and unzipped the top flap with the small square of mirror sewn in. Then I stared at myself without moving. I barely recognized my reflection. Even though I'd wanted to grow it long, my hair was shaggy and greasy, my skin was so pale I swear I could see through it, and the bruises left traces of green around my eyes and mouth. There was almost no resemblance to the boy in the picture I had just been looking at. I wondered then, for the first time, though I didn't mean to let the thought slip into my mind, if I would ever be that boy again.

CHAPTER 25

When a white man came into the restaurant one afternoon the following week, I stopped and stared. I was sure he'd come to rescue me, but I didn't know what to do. I felt my hands go sweaty and my legs tremble. I was afraid I was going to crash to the floor. But something drew me across the room toward him. Even though I knew Minh was the only one allowed to talk to customers, I couldn't stop myself.

"I'm Devon, from America. You've come to help me, right? They're keeping me downstairs. I can't ever leave," I said frantically.

The man looked up and spoke in a language I didn't understand. He sounded angry and waved me away. My throat closed up tight when I realized he hadn't come to save me at all.

"I don't belong here. Please help me," I pleaded as I tugged his arm.

He pushed me away, but I took hold of him again.

"Just tell someone where I am. Please, tell someone."

That was all I managed to say before Long pulled me away and dragged me downstairs. She slammed the door behind us and hit me until I curled into a tiny ball to protect myself.

"You do not speak to customers. Keep your mouth shut," she said over and over as she slapped me across the face and kicked my back.

"I won't do it again. I promise. Don't! Please don't!"

With each blow I begged her to stop, but the sound of my voice seemed to make her even angrier. So I stopped making any noise at all. I just curled up and let her hit me. I imagined I was a rock.

* * *

"You learn slow," Minh said that night while he pulled my bloody T-shirt over my head and examined the bruises on my back.

"I thought he was American. I thought he'd help us," I said through the pain.

"Lots of men from lots of different countries come here."

"Really?"

"Yes. Long's restaurant is famous."

"Do Americans come?"

"Sometimes."

"How can I get to the next one who speaks English?"

"Look at you – look at what Long did to you! How can you even think about trying again?" Minh said.

"I have to. I have to get out of here."

Minh sighed and shook his head.

"The men make their request to Long. You have no choice. And it wouldn't help. These men are not here to save us. I tried that too. I tried to get one of the regular men to go to my village in Vietnam. To tell my family where I was. I promised him money. I promised him anything. But he laughed at me. Then he told Long. I ended up looking worse than you."

"But it might be different with an American. An American would know I was kidnapped, that I don't belong," I insisted. "Then I could get us all out of here."

"None of us belong," Minh said bitterly.

"That's not what I meant," I said.

"American, Cambodian, European. They are all the same. They come here for the same reason."

I tried not to let Minh's talk discourage me, but over the following days I stopped thinking about how to escape, stopped looking for an opportunity to bolt. I stopped picturing home and thinking about what I'd do when I got back. I stopped thinking about how much I hated Lily and Long and the men. I stopped thinking. I went through the motions of living because I had no choice. I shoved my backpack under my cot. It was easier not to remember.

That's when the days started to blend into one another. Customers came and went, and I drank so many cups of calming tea that everything became a blur. The rain washed down the trough outside the window of our room every day, cleaning the garbage from the alley. But it was always back the next day with the same smell. The boys played dice every evening and sometimes I joined in or sometimes I sat on my cot with my face to the wall and my body a million miles away. I was so numb I didn't even notice when a new customer came in one day and requested me. As usual, Long sent me upstairs, and the man followed me to an empty room. I stood in the corner looking at my dirty bare feet and waited.

"Devon?" he said.

I dared to look up.

"You *are* Devon, right?"

I nodded and wondered why he was using my name. Most of the men didn't bother to call me by name. I wasn't sure any of them even knew my real name.

"Devon. I'm a police officer. I'm working undercover. I'm going to get you out of here and get you back home."

I didn't speak because I was used to saying nothing, thinking nothing. I had become as lifeless as Minh, An, and Hien.

"Devon, listen to me. Do you understand what I'm saying?"

"You're going to help me get out of here," I said without emotion.

"That's right. Are you ready?"

I nodded.

"Can you tell me if there's a back door? I need to know the layout. Do you understand, Devon?"

Each time he said my name it pulled me out of my trance a little more.

"There's no back door," I said finally. "Are you American?"

"I'm Vietnamese, but I studied in America. The police from America contacted me in Ho Chi Minh City. We've been searching a long time for you."

I looked into his face and my mind started to work, slowly, like an old bike that finally got its wheels oiled.

"Are we just going to walk out?"

"Quickly, yes. I have a partner downstairs. He's going to help us."

I pictured walking through the door with the man, then Long grabbing hold of me, pulling me back inside.

"Long will stop you."

"I think we can manage Long – if that's her name? We have a car outside waiting."

"And the others? You're bringing them too? Right?" Just the thought of leaving the others behind made my legs feel weak.

"How many are there?"

"Four boys downstairs and maybe six girls up here. The other boys are Vietnamese and some of the girls too, I think."

He swore once and then rubbed his chin.

"You can't leave the others," I pleaded. "You have to take us all."

"I didn't expect so many of you and the restaurant is packed. I'll need more back up," he said.

"Can you get more help?"

"I'll try. I'd have to come back. Are you sure that's what you want me to do?"

"How long will you take?"

"I don't know. A couple of hours?"

The thought of staying even one minute longer when escape was so close made my heart pound. I leaned over to steady myself. I knew what could happen in only a couple of hours, but I stood up and nodded. As badly as I wanted to walk out that very moment, I couldn't bear to think what Long might do to the others if I was rescued.

"I can't leave them. I just can't."

"Okay. I understand. When does the place close?" he asked.

"After dinner. Long doesn't stay open at night. She thinks it helps keep the cover of the restaurant."

"That should give me time to get help and get back. Now, Devon, listen closely. When you see me come in again I need you to do as I say. Will you have a chance to tell the other boys we're coming? You'll have to follow our commands quickly. Look at my face closely so you recognize me."

I studied his face. He had high-arching eyebrows, thick black hair, and a mole on his left cheek.

"Do you understand?"

"Yes," I said. I thought I understood, even though it was hard to piece it all together.

"You have to act like everything is normal. It's very important that Long doesn't catch on."

"Okay."

"I really hate to leave you here one more second, but I'll come back. I'm going to get you out of here – I promise," he said.

"Okay," I said softly, hoping I could in fact last a bit longer.

After he left I wasn't sure if I'd dreamed the whole thing or not. But I knew Long would be expecting me, so I went down the stairs as steadily as I could, hoping it would be the last time I ever made that trip.

When I got back to the restaurant, I tried to act normally. I kept my face to the floor and cleared dishes the way I always did. I stole glances at the other boys, wondering how I was going to warn them without getting caught. I managed to look at Long too, just to see if she looked suspicious. But she was perched by the front door as usual, smiling at customers and taking orders. Whenever the door opened and men came in I dared to search for the face of the undercover police officer and I wondered which of the men were coming to help us. But even after a couple of hours had passed, nothing seemed unusual. Everything was so normal, in fact, my stomach fell when Long locked the front door and took us back to our room for the night.

I waited until she was gone before I pulled Minh into the corner and whispered in his ear.

"We're going to be rescued! One of the customers told me. He's an undercover police officer from Vietnam. He was supposed to come back today, but he must have had trouble getting help. I'm sure he'll be back in the morning." I was so excited I could barely keep myself quiet. Minh looked at me with a strange expression.

"You have to stop making up fantasies."

"I'm not making it up. He's coming back to rescue us. When he comes in we have to do exactly what he says. Tell An and Hien what I just told you."

"You have seen too many movies."

"It's not a movie. It's real. He's coming tomorrow and we're getting out of here. You have to tell those guys what's going to happen so they can be ready."

"I am not going to tell them a lie."

"This is for real, Minh. We're going to get out of here! He wanted to take me today, but I said no, he had to take us all at once."

I wanted to shake him to make him understand.

"The only way out is to pay off your debt," he said sadly.

"You just wait and see," I said. "We're all going to get out of this hell hole. Finally."

I could not sit still that evening, and I'm sure An and Hien wondered what was going on. I had a hard time sleeping, and when morning finally came, I was the first one up. But when the day passed as usual and the police officer still hadn't come back, I dragged myself into the room and slumped onto my cot. Minh looked at me as if I was a stray dog, and I began to doubt myself. I wondered if the police officer had been hurt or the raid postponed. I began to wonder if I *had* imagined the whole thing, if I was losing it. I was sure I'd never see the sky again, the whole sky, not just a little patch through a barred window. I hadn't thought it was possible to feel any worse than I already did, but I was so low I didn't even care that the others heard me cry myself to sleep.

CHAPTER 26

Then it happened.

It was two days later than he promised, but the undercover police officer walked back into the restaurant. My heart jumped frantically inside my chest. I tried to meet his eyes so I could be sure, but he didn't even glance my way. Minh wasn't in the restaurant, and I realized with a sinking feeling that he must be upstairs. An and Hien were also gone and I hated myself for not keeping track of them. The man talked to Long and nodded toward me. Long smiled and whistled my signal. She loved it when customers returned.

The man followed me to the back. I could feel his breath and I could hear his feet clicking against the floor. I was confused because I hadn't seen any back-up men and I wondered if I was wrong again – if this man wasn't going to help after all. The weight of so much disappointment pressed down on me until I thought my lungs were collapsing. But when I took my fist step up, he directed me down to the basement instead, and I realized with a jolt that it was real.

"Go down and stay until I come for you. An officer is waiting there," he whispered quickly.

"What about the others?"

"They're down there already. Long thinks the men have been coming in to be with the boys, but they've been getting into position. Two of my men are upstairs. The police are going to come in the front any minute. Go – quick."

He pressed my back with his hand and I scurried downstairs.

Minh and the others were huddled in the corner. A man with a gun was crouched by the door and motioned for me to join them. I'd never seen a real gun before and I stopped dead. He pushed down on my shoulder until I squatted. Then I stayed low and scurried over beside Minh in case bullets started flying. None of us spoke – we just listened to the restaurant explode with noise. We heard screams and shouts. We heard a man trying to escape out a window, but a police officer was waiting there.

There were more shouts from upstairs, pounding feet. A girl cried for help. I could make out Long's angry voice in the chaos.

When the commotion upstairs settled, the undercover police officer re-appeared. He ducked through the low doorway and came over to us.

"Are you okay?" he asked me.

I nodded and tried to stand, but my legs were numb and I crumpled to the floor. He helped me up.

"We're going to get you home. Come on."

He started to lead me from the room, but I stalled.

"What about the others?"

"They're coming too. Back to Vietnam. First to the police station and then to a safe house."

I turned and motioned to the boys.

"*Lại đây!* They're taking us away from here."

"Are we in trouble?" Minh asked from the corner where he was still crouched with An and Hien.

"No! We're safe now. This is the man I told you about. Long is the one who is in trouble."

"But what will happen to us?"

"We're free. We're going home."

When Minh told the others what I was saying, An began to wail and shake his head.

"He is afraid to go home. He is too ashamed," Minh said.

The police officer kneeled beside the boys. He pulled them gently from the corner and spoke to them in Vietnamese. They relaxed when they heard him speaking their language.

"What did you tell them?" I asked when he stopped talking.

"I promised them nobody would hurt them ever again, that we'd get them cleaned up and fed and that we'd find them new clothes. I said they could figure out their futures another day."

I pulled on Minh's arm and motioned again for the boys to follow.

"Come on, please," I begged.

Minh looked up at me slowly. He studied my face for a moment before he let himself be led from the room. An and Hien followed because they were too afraid to be separated from him. An ducked down to scoop the dice from the floor, I dug my backpack out from under my cot, then we walked up the stairs and into the blinding sunlight.

CHAPTER 27

We stood outside the restaurant and shielded our eyes with our arms. We'd been living so long inside that the sun drilled into our eyes like lasers. Next to the brightness of the daylight, I noticed the feel of the outside air against my face. It felt fresh and soft, even though back home I would have found the same air smelly and damp. People stopped to watch what was going on and stared at me. I stepped behind Minh and closer to the wall as police officers pushed customers in handcuffs into waiting cars. The men didn't look at us, and I turned away so I wouldn't have to see them either. Finally, one of the police offers led us to an unmarked police van. There were already five girls sitting together on a seat, peeking from behind a bed sheet. Their eyes were red from crying and they clutched one another.

"Where's Tham?" I asked.

Nobody answered.

"Are these all the girls from upstairs?" I shouted as I banged on the side of the van.

The undercover police officer opened the back door and looked inside.

"There's at least one girl missing," I told him.

"I'll have someone look again," he said.

My heart was beating so hard I was sure the others could hear. I hoped something awful hadn't happened to her during the raid – that she hadn't gotten sick since I last saw her. But the undercover police officer appeared a few moments later with Tham beside him.

"She was under the bed," he said as he helped her into the back of the van. I was so relieved to see her I reached out to touch her, but she pulled away and looked around suspiciously.

"Don't be afraid," I said. "These men are here to help. They're going to take us back to Vietnam and to someplace safe."

"How can you be sure? How can you be sure we will not go someplace worse?" she said as she joined the other girls on the bench and pulled a corner of the sheet to cover herself. She spit the words so hard I couldn't believe she was the same girl who had helped me.

"Worse? What do you mean? We're *free* now!" I said.

"How do you know?"

"The police officer told me. He's going to take us to the police station in Ho Chi Minh City. Then to a safe house."

Tham snorted. "You are a silly boy, Devon. You cannot trust these men."

"Why not?"

"Maybe they are stealing us. Maybe they are taking us to another place. Maybe Long decided we are too old or ugly. Maybe she has prettier, younger girls to take our spots."

I didn't speak. I just stared at her with my mouth hanging open. Suddenly I noticed the heat rising up around me and the air felt too thick to breathe. Sweat was running down the side of my face and my T-shirt was damp. If only there was a breeze, I thought, if only there was a window we could open.

"It happens. Doesn't it, Qui?" Tham turned to another girl for backup. She wiped the sweat from her forehead with the back of her hand.

Qui nodded, then hid her face in the sheet.

"Qui used to work in Vietnam. Then one night Long's men raided the place. She was better off before she came here. At least they fed her well at the other place, and let them outside every day," Tham explained.

Suddenly I couldn't even swallow. I couldn't believe it was all a set-up and that I'd somehow helped to pull it off. Then the van lurched forward and the girls started to sob.

"Now there will be new men," Tham wailed. "Worse men. The kind who beat girls for fun."

I looked at Minh, but his face was as still as a mask and he was looking hard at his lap.

"Excuse me," I called up to the front.

The undercover police officer in the passenger seat turned around.

"Are you really police officers? Do you have badges or something?"

He pulled a badge out of the glove compartment and flashed it at us.

"We don't look it, but we *are* police officers. I'm sorry I didn't get a chance to introduce myself earlier, I'm Detective Pham. I work in Ho Chi

Minh City and I *promise* you are all safe now."

"Can you tell them too? They think you're taking them to another place like Long's."

He looked back at the girls and spoke in Vietnamese. Whatever he said seemed to calm them down because they stopped crying. An and Hien also seemed to relax and Minh let out the longest breath I've ever heard.

CHAPTER 28

Even though the van had air conditioning, with so many bodies sitting so close together, it was really hot and stinky. Nobody spoke as we drove through Phnom Penh, but we lurched and braced against the seats while the van jerked through the traffic. After a short drive we stopped and the girls grabbed each others' hands. Detective Pham turned to us.

"It's a bit of a drive back to Ho Chi Minh City. We thought you'd like something to eat and drink," he spoke in English and then in Vietnamese while the driver disappeared into a crowded market. I looked out the front window, but the others shrank down in their seats.

The driver returned a few moments later and handed back bottles of water, rice patties, a large bag of peanuts, and three bunches of bananas. I grabbed a bottle of water and chugged it down, and the boys followed my lead. I tore off a banana peel and shoved the fruit into my mouth. The sweetness of it made my teeth tingle the way too much candy does on Halloween night. When they saw the food, the girls didn't wait long either, and soon we were all eating and drinking. We were so busy filling our mouths in fact, nobody noticed when the van started moving again. After I'd eaten a rice patty, four bananas, several handfuls of peanuts, and drank two bottles of water, I fell asleep against Minh's shoulder.

There was a short delay at the border, but then we went right to Ho Chi Minh City. We got to the police station after dark and followed the police officers into a small, brightly lit room. There was a table and chairs, but the others sat together on the floor in the far corner and I joined them. I leaned against the wall with my arms resting on my knees. A uniformed officer came in with more bottles of water and handed them out. I splashed the water on my face then drank the rest in one gulp. I wasn't sure I'd ever stop being thirsty. Detective Pham came to crouch on the floor beside me. The others pressed closer together like a herd of sheep.

"I'm really sorry for the delay, but we had some trouble with the chief of police in Phnom Penh. I don't think he liked us being in his city. He tried to tell me that Long's didn't exist."

"I was afraid you weren't coming back," I said and rested my head against the wall.

"I'm sorry you had to spend another day – another minute – in there."

"I'm just so tired right now."

"You can sleep soon. We found a house with enough beds for all of you."

"The others," I nodded to the girls huddled together, "they still think they're in trouble. They think you're going to arrest them."

"I'll talk to them."

"I don't think they trust police officers at all," I said quietly.

Just then the door opened and an officer stepped in with food. He handed us each a packet of chicken and rice along with some chopsticks. I'd gone so long without feeling full, my hunger seemed endless. I didn't think any amount of food would satisfy me. So like the others, I put the packet up to my chin and used the chopsticks to shovel the food into my mouth. Detective Pham watched while we ate. He looked sad and tired, but relieved. I wondered how long he'd been awake, working to get us out of that place.

The next police officer who came in brought changes of clothes. The girls pulled baggy track pants and t-shirts over themselves shyly. Minh, An, Hien and I ripped off our smelly shirts and pants as privately as we could, then pulled on clean ones. I buried my face in my shirt. I never knew the smell of lemon laundry detergent could make me feel so good.

Finally Detective Pham turned to me. "We want to bring in a doctor to examine each of you. Then we'll take you all to the safe house where you can have showers and sleep. It's a nice place, and everyone can stay until we get them home or find them places to live. But we don't want to scare anyone, so maybe if you'd be an example, the others will follow. Can we have the doctor look at you first?"

"In here or another room?"

"In here, where the others can see that they don't have to be afraid. It's only a very basic check this time. The rest will come later in private."

"Will I have to undress?"

"No, it's just to look for any obvious problems. You'll have to have a thorough examination later. At that point, they'll want to take blood tests, x-rays, a full physical, that sort of thing."

Even though I could only picture Uncle Tho in my mind when I thought of a Vietnamese doctor, Detective Pham made me feel safe. So I agreed and the doctor came in. He took my temperature and looked in my mouth, eyes, and ears. Using Detective Pham as a translator he asked me questions while he listened to my heart and lungs, took my blood pressure, and felt under my jaw and armpits. I tried to look relaxed so the others wouldn't be afraid, but it was hard letting a stranger touch me like that after my time at Long's. He made notes on a pad of paper and then weighed me, measured my height, and tested my reflexes. When he was finished, I sat at the table. Next he examined Minh, then An, Hien, Tham, and the other girls.

Detective Pham sat down beside me.

"Am I okay?"

"We'll know better later."

"When can I go home?"

"As soon as possible. I have some calls to make tomorrow. We have to get you a new passport. Or maybe under the circumstances you can travel without one. But I'll have to contact the Embassy to find out."

"Thanks," I said.

"What about the others? Is there anything we can do to help them right now?" he asked.

I turned to Minh.

"What about you, Minh? Is there anything you need tonight?"

Minh paused. I could tell he had something he wanted to say.

"Just tell him," I encouraged.

"Does he have a telephone?" Minh whispered to me. "My uncle has a phone, and I want to call him."

Detective Pham must have overheard because he nodded and smiled, then left the room. When he returned he had a cell phone. Detective Pham helped Minh press in the numbers then handed it to him. Minh took it carefully, like it might be hot, then put it to his ear and waited. I leaned close to listen. The ringing seemed to go on for hours, but then Minh started to talk. His voice was so quiet he had to say his name several times before he finally spoke up. By the time the conversation ended though, Minh was sitting a little straighter. I even saw him smile. I wished I had someone to call too, but I couldn't imagine calling Vic and with Dad dead, there was no one else I trusted.

After Minh called home, I think An and Hien finally believed they were safe because they lifted their heads and looked around the room. Then, one by one, the girls began to trust Detective Pham and the other police officers, and they smiled shyly. Tham was the last to be won over, but eventually she sat at the table next to me.

"Why does he want to help us?" she asked, nodding at Detective Pham.

I turned to Detective Pham, even though I knew he heard her question. "She wants to know why you're helping us."

He turned and spoke directly to her.

"Because I'm disgusted that there are grown men who hurt children, and I want to do everything I possibly can to stop it. I hate the fact that there are people who sell children for profit and I want them punished."

"But how did you find us? And why us? I am sure there are others you could have helped."

Minh translated for the others while Detective Pham paused to put his thoughts together.

"It's a long story and I don't know everything that happened in America, but I do know we were looking for Devon, to start. We'd been alerted by the National Center for Missing and Exploited Children that he was missing somewhere in Ho Chi Minh City and possibly in a brothel that fronted as a restaurant. We had a picture and description and contacted all the police stations in Vietnam. Then someone on our Sex Crimes team saw an ad posted on the Internet for a redheaded boy for sale."

"The Internet?" I managed to whisper.

"Yes," Detective Pham said soberly.

The room started to spin and I rested my forehead on the table. I'd never considered the idea that Long would have advertised me on the Internet.

Detective Pham nodded. "It's horrible, I know. I see things every day that make me so sick. But if it wasn't for that ad, we might never have found you."

I fought to breathe. It felt as if the air had been knocked out of me, like the time Cody dared me to grind the handrail at school and I wiped out. Tham reached to touch my shoulder, but I shrugged her off. Detective Pham continued.

"We could tell the ad had been posted from Phnom Penh so we went undercover to find out more. We soon heard about 'Red,' an American boy who worked at Long's restaurant, and we were pretty certain it was you, Devon."

Tham leaned down and spoke softly to me.

"I wonder if Long will ever find out it was your red hair that got her arrested."

I didn't know, but I hoped it would get Lily arrested too.

CHAPTER 29

I was in Vietnam for a week before I flew home. I stayed in the safe house with the others and shared a bedroom with Minh, An, and Hien. The girls were split up between two other bedrooms and we all shared the living room and kitchen.

When we had first arrived, Detective Pham showed us around. He introduced us to a lady, who immediately went to the fridge and got a plate of fresh fruit and bread rolls. We inhaled the food and I wondered how long it would take before we stopped eating like animals. Then, even though it was late, the others went to the living room to watch TV. But I took my backpack and went to the bathroom.

The bathroom was so clean it sparkled like a commercial for household cleaners. There was a shower and sink, a toilet, and a rack of towels. I pulled down a towel and rubbed my face against it. I hadn't seen a bath towel for so long I'd forgotten they even existed. There was a mirror above the sink, and I examined my face up close. My freckles had faded and there were still faint outlines of bruises around my eyes. I ran my fingers along my cheekbones and my jaw, trying to recognize myself. It had been months since I'd seen my face so clearly.

I let the shower get hot, then I peeled off my clothes and stepped in. I lathered up the bar of soap and washed myself over and over. I wondered if I'd ever scrub the smell of the basement off my skin. Then I heaped toothpaste on my toothbrush and brushed my teeth for probably twenty minutes straight. When I finally felt clean, I combed the knots out of my hair, dressed, then changed my mind and had another shower. Steam poured into the hallway when I unlocked the door and stepped out.

The others were still watching TV when I arrived back in the living room. I watched for a minute, but I couldn't understand anything that was being said, so I went to bed and stretched out on the clean white sheets below the open window. I was so tired I thought I could sleep forever. But I was afraid to close my eyes in case it was all a dream.

"Are you okay?" Detective Pham asked from the door.

I turned my head and nodded.

"Just thinking," I said.

"You must have a lot on your mind," he said as he stepped inside the room and sat on Minh's bed.

"Yeah. Right now I can't stop thinking about what happened to ...my dad's ashes." I knew it was the least of my worries, but somehow I needed to know they were safe, that Lily hadn't thrown them out or something.

"Let me see what I can find out, okay?"

I nodded. I doubted he'd ever be able to find them, but I was glad he cared enough to try.

"Everyone seems to be settled in, so I'm going to go now. I'll be back in the morning. If you need anything, just ask one of the staff members. Someone will always be here. They can reach me if they need to."

"I think I'll be okay."

"Sleep well," he said and left.

When I opened my eyes the next morning, I stood right up and stared out the window. I couldn't get enough of looking at the sky. I stared at it for twenty minutes before I went to the back door to see if it was locked. It wasn't. We were free to go outside whenever we felt like it. That first morning, I went out to the back yard ten times in ten minutes, just because I could. One of the house ladies came to the door to see what was going on. I had just stepped in and was about to go out again when I saw her and I apologized. Tham was there too.

"You go in and out more than a cat," Tham said and smiled.

The neighborhood around the safe house was quiet; there were no cars honking, no people yelling. My favorite thing was relaxing in the hammock and looking up at the leaves on the tree. Tham called the tree *cay trung ca* and, like me, she loved to sit under it just so she could be outside. We spent a lot of time together that week.

Three women ran the house and worked in overlapping shifts. Like Detective Pham promised, we were never left on our own. They cooked and cleaned and asked us all the time if we needed anything. I think they wanted to fatten us up because they brought us snacks between every meal and smiled when we ate everything. I heard someone look in on us each night, and more than once I was caught in a hug by the lady who worked the afternoon shift.

The safe house was a busy place. People came and went constantly and everyone wanted me for something. A doctor came the first day to do complete medical examinations on each of us. He took me into the office first and had me change into in a hospital gown. I hated being almost naked in front of him, and when he touched me, my heart raced and I froze.

"I'm sorry, this is going to be cold," he said when he pressed the stethoscope to my chest.

I don't think he realized it wasn't the cold that made me flinch and shut my eyes tight.

He took blood samples and a throat swab and gave me a little cup to pee into. He asked me questions about what had happened, and when I didn't answer, he prompted me. I forced myself to remember everything I'd worked so hard to forget. Some of his questions made me angry, and I wished more than anything that he'd just let me go outside again. When he .finished he told me I'd have to come into the clinic the next day for X-rays and that when he got my results, he'd write a report for my doctor back home. The whole thing made my stomach ache, and I paced the backyard for an hour before I calmed down enough to lie in the hammock.

Social workers came to speak to us, both as a group and alone. I think they were frustrated by how little any of us said or even wanted to say. The police came too and asked us questions with the hopes of tracking down family members and the criminals who had sold us in the first place. I told them as much as I could about Lily and gave them our home address and phone number, hoping they'd arrest her before she found out I was free and tried to hide.

Detective Pham came each day to talk to me about going home and about the progress he was making getting my flight and passport arranged. When I thought about getting on a plane and back to America, I was excited. But I was scared too and a little hesitant about leaving the others. Detective Pham made arrangements for someone to come and fly back with me – a detective who worked closely with victims like me and who had been working on my case from America. He told me I was being placed with a foster family. I had no idea what that would be like, so I tried not to let myself think about it too much.

It didn't take long before Minh and Hien made arrangements to go home, but An couldn't decide. Since Long was his cousin, he knew everyone in his village would hear about her arrest and realize what had happened to him. He wasn't sure he could face it. Minh and I encouraged him to go home and see his family anyway.

"He's still not sure," Minh said. "He says there will be a lot of talk."

I looked at An. His face was pale.

"Tell him to let them talk," I said to Minh. "At least he has a mother to go home to. If I had a mother, I'd go see her."

"He thinks they will blame him."

"It's not his fault!" I shouted. My anger surprised me. I sounded brave, but I wasn't sure I believed what I was saying.

Three of the younger girls were going home, but the two older girls were staying in the safe house until they found jobs and had enough money to support themselves. Tham was the oldest and hadn't made up her mind by the time I left.

"I have only an aunt back home. I have been gone too long. I am sure she has forgotten about me. Maybe I will come to America one day and find you. Maybe I need to start fresh," she said.

"'I don't know what it will be like when I get home," I confessed. "I haven't got anyone now so I'm going to live with a foster family. I don't even know who they are." I shivered at the thought.

"At least there is someone for you," Tham said sadly.

We were sitting together on the hammock in the shade of the *cay trung ca* tree on my second to last day, and my head was so jammed up with thoughts and feelings it was hard to keep the conversation going.

"I hate to think I'll never see you again," I said when I noticed the silence that hung between us.

She looked at me a minute then leaned over to hug me. "When I need you, I will find you."

"But what about when I need you?"

"You will be fine," she said. "You must be lucky to have so many people looking for you."

I passed her a folded square of paper with my name, city and e-mail address printed in block letters. "When you find a computer to use, send me an e-mail."

"But I have never even used a computer," she protested.

"It's easy. You'll learn."

"I have too much to learn. I will not be able to do it all."

"You will."

Though I'd never asked her how she came to Long's, I'd learned the story from Qui. Tham had been begging on the street one day when Long offered her a place to live and a job at the restaurant. Tham didn't know she wouldn't be allowed to leave once she set foot inside.

"I never got to say it, but thank you for helping me that day," I said.

"Thank you for helping me," she said.

That night, the boys watched as I packed my bag. It didn't take long to sort through my things and when I was done, I picked out something to give each of them. I gave my skateboarding magazines to Hien, my cap to Minh, and my flashlight to An.

"I wish I had something better to give you," I said to Minh.

"What do you mean?" Minh asked as he pulled the cap over his newly cut hair. "I have not had a present in a long time."

When I finally went to bed, I lay for hours in the darkness. I thought about going home and wondered what it would be like, what my foster family would be like, how I'd get along without Dad. It was hard to think of leaving, knowing I'd never see the people in the house around me, the people I'd begun to care so much about. I was finally drifting off when someone coughed in another room, then one of the girls cried out in her sleep. I wondered if it was Tham.

The next morning I hugged everyone before I climbed in the car with Detective Pham – even the social workers and the women who ran the house came to say goodbye. I was the first one to leave and that made it even more difficult. As we pulled away, everyone stood at the front gate and waved. Minh ran alongside the car until we picked up speed, and Tham wiped her eyes with one hand and waved with the other. I leaned out the window and waved frantically back and as I did, the tears flowed. I was relieved to think they would be the last tears I would shed in Vietnam.

CHAPTER 30

On the way to the airport I rubbed my hands on my new jeans and looked out the window. I was glad I'd never have to deal with so much commotion again. We passed by a man selling fish from a long, flat wagon, and I thought of the day we arrived at Lily's family's apartment – how both Dad and I had gawked like little kids. That was the last day Dad was ever outside. The busy street was the last thing he'd seen before he laid down in that small back bedroom. Whenever I thought about going home without Dad, a sharp pain stabbed my chest. I doubted I would ever really feel at home again.

When we got to the airport, I held my backpack tightly and stayed close to Detective Pham. He led me through the crowds to a small private waiting room. Detective Pearson, the police escort from America, was already waiting for us. He stood up when we stepped inside. He was a tall, balding man with a thick black mustache and brown eyes. He was wearing jeans and a blue-striped golf shirt and he smelled like deodorant. We said hello and then I sat quietly while they spoke about the flight and Ho Chi Minh City and Detective Pearson's night in the hotel.

"How are you feeling?" Detective Pham asked me finally, when he got ready to leave.

"Okay, I guess," I said. "Nervous."

"That's understandable. Now remember, Detective Pearson can get in touch with me if he needs to."

I looked at the floor and wondered what else I should say. "Thank you" didn't seem quite right and I couldn't think of anything else.

"Have a good flight," he said finally, when he realized I wasn't going to speak.

"Okay," I said and looked up.

"Take care of yourself."

"I will," I managed to say.

He put out his hand and I offered mine in return. His grip was tight and I could feel that he wanted to say more. But he didn't. He just patted me on the back, then opened the door and disappeared.

I knew I was safe, but I still felt nervous being alone with a stranger in such a small room. Detective Pearson must have sensed how I was feeling because he asked me if I was hungry.

"I could always eat," I admitted.

"Do you want to wait here while I go find something, or do you want to come with me?"

"Um, I'll wait here," I said.

He nodded and left me in the sitting room. I found a computer magazine in the recycling bin and flipped through it just to keep my mind busy.

When he returned a few minutes later he handed me a McDonald's bag. Inside was a hamburger, fries, and a Coke. I tore open the hamburger wrapper and tried to chew slowly, but it was hard. Before long I realized I was slurping up the last of the soda.

That's when Detective Pearson rummaged in his briefcase and handed me the latest issue of *Thrasher* magazine.

"This might be a little more interesting for you," he said, glancing at what I'd been reading.

"Thanks," I said. "This one's my favorite."

"I heard you were into skateboarding, so I brought some back issues too. My nephew's a fan."

I flipped through the magazine until Detective Pearson's cell phone rang. Someone was calling to let us know it was time to board the plane. He stood up and handed me a brown hoodie.

"Pull the hood up and look bored. That way everyone will think you're my son and they won't take any notice. I don't want anyone to recognize you."

When we left the waiting room, I was glad to be moving again. Sitting made me feel edgy. The plane was already full when we walked on, and we sat in the very first seats where there was lots of leg room. As soon as we put on our seatbelts, the flight attendants did their safety check and the engines roared to life. My homecoming was getting closer, and I still had no idea what to expect.

""Have you met my foster parents?" I asked as the plane pulled away from the gate and began to taxi toward the runway. I couldn't put off facing my new reality any longer.

"I have. I met them before I came. They're very nice – Joy and Ted. They have two adult children and one little foster girl right now."

"So they're going to, like, take care of me?"

"Yeah, they look after kids who need homes."

"Will I have my own bedroom?"

"Yes, all to yourself. I've seen it. It's blue and it has a big window looking out over the front yard."

"And it'll be, like, living in a regular home?"

"Sure. They're a normal family. They eat meals and go to work and they'll take you to school and help you with your homework. All the regular stuff. Just like real parents."

I thought about Dad's relaxed rules before Lily came along, and I wondered if I'd be ready for anything "regular."

"Do they get paid?"

"They get an allowance to buy you clothes and money for food. But they don't do it for the money. It's not a job to them."

"But they take in other kids?"

"One or two when someone needs them. But it's not a group home or anything."

"Where do they live?"

"Not far from your school, actually. The children's services worker said they were one of their best families and assured me you'd be happy there."

"And if I'm not?"

"Then they'll try to find you a place where you *are* happy."

"What if I'm never happy?"

"There's no rush. There're going to be a lot of people helping you, including me."

The airplane began to rumble and shake, and when it finally took off, I pressed myself against the seat. I watched out the window as the city fell away. I watched the airport and the city streets become one massive circuit board. Then Vietnam disappeared beneath the clouds.

"If you're up to it, I'd like to show you something," Detective Pearson said when the plane leveled off and there was nothing more for me to look at out the window.

He opened up his laptop and we spent the next two hours looking at newspaper articles and newscasts reporting my disappearance and the frantic search for me. I was stunned. I couldn't connect what was in the news with the reality I'd just escaped. They didn't have anything right, except my name and age.

"You have to be prepared for this when we get off the plane. Everyone wants to know what happened to you. People have been following your story. Even when there was no news there was something in the paper about you. Your teachers, your friends, your neighbors, everyone's been interviewed about you."

Detective Pearson even showed me an article that quoted Vic saying: "He's my best friend – I know he didn't run away. He'd have e-mailed me by now if he could. Something's definitely wrong."

I tried, but I couldn't picture Vic clearly, and I wondered how I'd ever face him again – how he'd feel about me when he found out what I'd done ... what they made me do.

"But how did you know to start looking for me?"

"Your friend, Vic, actually. He got suspicious when you didn't come home after two months like you were supposed to. When he found out your stepmother was home and you weren't, he had his parents contact the police and we started the investigation."

"She's not my stepmother."

"I'm sorry."

"I hate her. I never want to see her again."

"She hasn't been very nice to us either. Hasn't been the least bit cooperative – even once we had her in custody."

"Lily was in jail?"

"She *is* in jail."

"Forever?"

"We don't know what's going to happen. They're still trying to sort out her real identity and her past. There are some major discrepancies about who she says she is and what she says she's been doing."

"What about Quan and Sang? Where are they? Who's taking care of them?"

"They're with a foster family. And in a new school. They're okay."

As much as I hated Lily and as much as I'd resented the twins when they moved in, I felt sad when I thought of Quan and Sang – when I realized their lives had been messed up by her too.

"Did Lily tell you where I was?" I asked finally.

"Not to start. She said you'd run away while you were in Vietnam. She said you were so upset over your father dying that you had a fight with her then ran away. She told us she looked for you everywhere but that she had to come home finally."

I gritted my teeth until my jaw hurt. "That's a lie. She sold me to Long on purpose. And she knew exactly what would happen to me. I'm sure of it."

"We figured the first part out pretty fast since there weren't any reports of a missing American boy in Ho Chi Minh City, or anywhere else in Vietnam, for that matter. But Sang led us to Long finally. It took us a while to get anything out of him, but eventually he let it slip. Quan wouldn't say a word."

"But how did Sang know I was there?"

"He didn't. But we found out he and Quan had been there before they came to America, so we thought it might be a possibility. We don't think Lily sold you as much as she traded you. Their freedom for yours. The problem was, we didn't know what city Long was in."

"Wait! Quan and Sang were at Long's?" My throat clamped shut and I struggled to breathe.

"Apparently Lily left them with a friend when she came to America, but the friend sold them. When Lily finally tracked them down, Long refused to give them up unless Lily paid a lot of money."

My head spun while I tried to piece together everything I knew with what Detective Pearson was telling me. I was so nauseous I felt like I did the time I went on the Gravitron at the fair with Vic and Eric.

"Why didn't Lily just go to the police about the twins?"

"Lily said Long threatened her, said Long had men who would kill her *and* the boys if she told the police or didn't pay off the debt. Lily then promised to deliver you."

"So she planned the whole thing? She tricked Dad into going to Vietnam so she could sell me?"

"That's what we think"

"Did she ... kill Dad ... on purpose?" I choked.

"What do you mean?"

By then I was crying so it was hard to speak. But I swallowed my tears. "Did she poison him ...on purpose? With her tea?"

"We don't know yet. We're still trying to figure that out."

CHAPTER 31

By the time dinner was served, I'd stopped crying and was starving again. I ate my food and Detective Pearson's, plus I drank two cans of Coke and inhaled two desserts that the flight attendant brought me. The sugar rush made me dizzy, but that didn't stop me.

"Do you have any potato chips?" I asked when the flight attendant came by to check on us later.

"Let me see what I can find," she said. She returned moments later with several small bags of chips and pretzels.

When my stomach finally felt like there was something in it, I yawned. My eyes felt dry and my eyelids were heavy. I sat up straight and flipped through the skateboarding magazines, so I wouldn't fall asleep. I was afraid of dreaming about being back at Long's. Eventually, however, when my eyes hurt from reading, I gave in and closed them. I promised myself it would only be for a few minutes while I listened to music on the headphones. Over the songs I could hear Detective Pearson tapping away on his laptop. I wondered what he was working on and whether or not I should ask to check my e-mail, but the thought slipped away and I fell asleep.

When I awoke, I could tell from the angle of the airplane that we were approaching the airport. The music was still playing in my ears and I pulled off the headphones in a panic.

"We're home?" I asked Detective Pearson with my heart pounding.

"We'll be at the gate in about twenty minutes."

I looked at the city below us. All I could see were millions of lights in the darkness. I could make out the highway slithering like a snake through the city and the downtown high-rises jagged against the horizon. I couldn't believe that somewhere in all of that darkness there were people I knew who were watching TV and eating dinner. I couldn't believe that Vic was down there, that Eric and Cody were in their houses with their families, without the faintest idea that I was on my way home.

"Now I go to my foster family?" I asked when the plane bumped on the runway.

"First we have to get you through customs. I hope the media didn't find out you're on this plane," he said with what I thought was a touch of dread.

"What happens if the media finds out?"

"They mob you and then your picture will be in every newspaper in the morning. Then you won't get a moment's privacy. But if it works according to *my* plan, they won't find out for a few days that you're home."

"What does the foster family know about me?"

"They know the basic circumstances," Detective Pearson said and for the first time I could hear the hesitation in his voice.

"Do they know my dad died?"

"Yes."

"And that Lily ... uh ... left me ... in Vietnam."

"Yes."

"Do they know she's in jail?"

"Uh huh."

"Do they know about Long?"

"Yes."

"And what happened in Cambodia?"

"In general terms."

The image of Long's face jumped into my mind and I felt acid rise up the back of my throat. I understood suddenly what An feared about going home. My heart raced and I couldn't catch my breath. I gasped for air and my eyes watered. I was fine one minute, then my body went haywire. I didn't understand what was happening to me.

"Breathe, Devon. Take a deep breath and exhale slowly. We're going to get you help for this – everything you need until you learn to cope. But just breathe for now."

Detective Pearson's voice was calm and I held onto it like a lifeline.

"Breath in one, two, three, and exhale one, two, three, four."

He adjusted the vents above us to let in the cool air, and I gulped it like a fish on land.

"Just keep breathing. That's it. You're doing great," he said, counting through a few rounds of deep breaths until I got control of my body again.

"Does everybody in America know every freakin' thing that happened to me?" I asked with so much anger that I scared myself.

"Not yet. And not if I have it my way. Not if we can keep the media away from you. Everyone will want to know you're home safe. But we can hold a press conference in a day or two. For now we just need to get you home."

Home. I couldn't even picture home so it was a meaningless word. But I didn't have long to dwell on what it might be like because the airplane pulled to a stop. Detective Pearson stood up and rummaged through the overhead compartment. He handed me a winter coat.

"It's pretty cold out there. You're going to need something warm."

I pulled on the coat and reminded myself that it was winter again, that I'd missed most of spring, summer, and fall. I wondered what else I'd missed.

He reached over, pulled my hood up to cover my face, and put his hand on my shoulder. "Let's do it then."

As we stepped off the plane, the stewardess caught my eye and said, "Welcome home, Devon."

I couldn't believe she knew my name.

Part 3: Joy

CHAPTER 32

The closer we got to my foster family's house, the bigger the lump in my throat grew. I strained to recognize where we were and eventually we started passing familiar streets and storefronts. Detective Pearson's car smelled like a pine-scented air freshener, and when I couldn't stand it any longer, I rolled down the window.

"Sorry it reeks in here. My dog loves the car, but he's not one for taking baths." He smiled and I knew he was trying to lighten the mood. I held my hands together to keep them from trembling.

"What kind of dog do you have?" I managed to ask, just to keep him talking – just so the darkness would be filled with something besides my fear.

"A beagle. They're famous for smelling bad."

"Are we almost there?" I asked when we passed within a block of my school.

"Three more streets, then we turn right."

"We're near our townhouse," I said as I wondered who lived there now and what happened to all our things. I didn't have a chance to ask though, because Detective Pearson pulled into a driveway and turned off the car. He looked over at me and my face must have given away my nervousness because he said, "Don't worry. Joy and Ted are great." Then he got out and came to help me out.

The house was narrow and tall and made of red brick. It had a separate garage down the side of the house and a porch wrapped around one corner. As we walked up the front steps, I looked up at the second-story windows and wondered which was going to be my bedroom. The door opened before Detective Pearson even rang the bell. Standing before us was a thin woman with soft lines around her eyes and mouth. She had short graying hair and was wearing jeans, a white turtleneck, and a dark blue sweater.

"Devon! Come in!" she said with more energy than I would have expected from someone so small.

I stepped in and almost bumped into her when she moved to let Detective Pearson inside too. It felt strange that she knew so much about me while I knew nothing about her.

"I'm Joy. It's so nice to meet you."

She shook my hand warmly then took our coats and ushered us into the living room.

"Please, have a seat while I hang these up."

When she opened the closet door, something hard fell on the floor.

"Just Ted's hockey stick. I'll never know why he has to leave it right here," she said.

Detective Pearson and I sat on the couch and exchanged glances. He smiled and I studied the carpet. Even though I knew I was back in my own city, I felt as though I was in a brand new country. It wasn't just that I was in a strange house – I couldn't figure out if it was early evening or the middle of the night. I even had to stop and think what year it was.

"What time is it anyway?" I asked.

"Ten," Detective Pearson said.

"Really? What day is it?"

"Friday."

"I can't believe I didn't even know," I said quietly. "I'm really spaced out."

"I'm sure you'll feel better after a good night's sleep," Detective Pearson said.

The living room was warm and crowded with comfortable couches and armchairs, fleece blankets, and pillows. Everything seemed so soft and inviting compared to Vietnam. There was a box of toys under the bay window by a rocking chair and a stack of sports magazines on the coffee table. A Christmas tree was already decorated in the corner. I wasn't sure I was ready for the happiness of Christmas.

"Would either of you like a drink or something to eat?" Joy asked as she perched on the arm of the couch.

"I could use a cup of tea, thanks," Detective Pearson said. "Devon, would you like something?"

The words came from across the room, but they didn't register the first time. When I heard him repeat the question I looked up.

"Would you like something, Devon? What would you like to drink?"

If he didn't ask me directly, I wouldn't have asked for anything. But he didn't leave me a choice, so I asked for a glass of milk.

"Coming right up!" Joy sprang to her feet and disappeared again.

She came back with our drinks and a plate of cookies. I didn't touch one until she put the plate right under my nose.

"Please help yourself. Or would you like something else? Some bacon and eggs? A grilled cheese sandwich?"

As she spoke she fidgeted with the bottom of her sweater.

"I'm good with cookies. Thanks."

I looked around the room and tried to think of it as my new home while the two of them talked about the flight, the media, school, therapy, my schedule, and my appointments over the coming days.

"There are only two weeks of school left before the holidays," Joy said, "so we thought Devon might like to wait until the new year to go back. Of course, it's up to him. First he just needs to get used to living here with us." Joy smiled at me, and I wondered if she would be the kind of mother Dad always wanted me to have.

It felt as though they were talking about someone else. I couldn't connect the words they were saying to myself. What did my life have to do with the media, therapists, social services? I was so exhausted and overwhelmed I could barely recognize my own hands resting in my lap.

"I'm sorry, Devon," Joy said. "I've been so rude. It's late and I'm sure you're tired. Would you like to see your room and maybe get some sleep?"

Her voice was soft. I wondered if she always spoke so quietly or if she was worried about waking someone.

I nodded. More than anything I wanted to be alone.

She stood up and headed for the stairs. I followed and Detective Pearson fell into step behind me.

"I think you'll find everything you need," she said. "But if not, *please* come and ask. Our room is just across the hall. The bathroom is right next door. I've left out a new toothbrush and washcloth. There are plenty of clean towels on the shelf if you want a shower."

"I think I'll just go to bed."

"Of course. And promise you'll ask if you need anything or if you can't sleep. Just knock on our door and don't worry about waking us. We're so glad you're finally here."

"I'll be okay," I said, though I wasn't really so sure.

She opened the door to my bedroom and let me walk in ahead of her. My jaw dropped when I looked around. The room was filled with my things – my X-Box and games, my skateboard, my baseball glove, my music and skateboard magazines, the new bedding Dad had bought me when we moved into the townhouse. I had to catch my breath.

"The landlord packed up your things when Lily was taken into custody. But he needed to rent out the unit, so he put everything into a storage unit. We brought some of it here, to make you feel at home. We even have some of your clothes in the closet. You'll have to see if they still fit. When you're ready to look through everything, we can go over to see what else you want," Joy said.

I looked around the room as if it was a museum. My hands reached out automatically to touch everything, as if to convince my mind it was all real. I stopped when I saw a framed picture of me and Dad on the dresser. It was from the summer before he met Lily. We were on a fishing trip with one of his friends from the meat works. We didn't catch much that day, just a few throw-away carp, but I suddenly remembered it as one of the best afternoons of my life. I stared at Dad's face. Even though I still had the photobooth pictures in my wallet, I'd started to forget the details: the scar above his left eyebrow, the exact shape of his lips, the way the laugh lines stretched out from the corners of his eyes. It was the only face more familiar than my own.

Beside the picture was a wooden box like the one Lily had shown me in the restaurant in Ho Chi Minh City. I looked up hopefully at Joy and she nodded.

"We found it at the storage unit," she said.

CHAPTER 33

It was the smell of frying bacon that made it into my dream the next morning and made me start to understand just how messed up I really was.

Dad and I were at the diner down the street from our apartment, having our traditional Sunday-morning breakfast.

"Sausage or bacon with the special today?" Dad asked me before the waitress came to take our order.

"Sausage," I said. "No wait, make it bacon."

"That's my boy. I sure have missed our Sundays together. Don't stay away so long next time," he said.

"What do you mean?" I asked, confused, while my mind pulled me into the day. I jolted fully awake when I remembered where I was.

Now that I was going to see everything that had belonged to us together – the ballpark, the mall, the diner – I wasn't sure I was ready to face any of it.

I dressed and went down to the kitchen.

"Devon! You're up! I hope I didn't make too much noise." Joy was at the stove wearing an apron and smiled when she saw me standing at the door. I didn't have a smile to return, but she didn't seem to mind.

She was flipping the bacon and she pulled her hand back when the grease spattered.

"No, I didn't hear anything. I just woke up a little while ago."

I glanced at a clock on the wall. It was ten-thirty.

"What day is it again?" I asked.

"Saturday. Kimmy and Ted should be back from swimming lessons any minute." She reached behind her and untied the apron, then tossed it on the counter.

"I have to apologize. I don't like anyone to see me wearing that thing. It's old fashioned, even for me."

"That's okay. Dad used to wear one too."

"No kidding?"

"Yeah, he was a good cook, but he was a really messy one. He hated ruining his pants all the time."

I heard the front door open and moments later a little girl bounced into the kitchen. Her cheeks were pink from being out in the cold, and her long hair was tangled from wearing a hat. She stopped when she saw me.

"Kimmy, this is Devon. Devon, this is Kimmy," Joy said from across the room.

"Hi, Kimmy," I said quietly.

The girl walked over and held out her hand for me to shake, which seemed like a weird thing for someone so young to do.

"Hi, Devon. I'm very pleased to meet you. Do you know how to play Monopoly?"

Joy laughed before I could answer. "Kimmy's just discovered board games. We're stuck on Monopoly right now. Kimmy, I'm sure Devon's played Monopoly before. Please don't bother him to play right now."

Ted came into the kitchen next. He reminded me of Hans Solo, but his hair was cut short and he didn't have a scar on his chin. Joy introduced us and then told us to sit down. She put a plate heaped with fried eggs, bacon, and toast in front of me. I tried hard to eat slowly so she wouldn't think I was rude.

"More toast?" she asked a few minutes later when my plate was empty.

"Yes, please."

"Juice or milk?"

"Milk, please," I said.

She poured me a glass of milk and put two more pieces of toast on my plate, then handed me a jar of raspberry jam.

"You have an appointment with the doctor after breakfast, and then your social worker is going to stop by to meet you. After that you can do whatever you'd like – your choice. Anything specific you'd like to do?"

I couldn't imagine what I could possibly want to do, so I shook my head.

"Maybe you'd like to play Monopoly with me," Kimmy suggested.

"Sweetie, you'll have to give Devon a few days to settle in before he'll feel like playing games, I think," Ted said.

"So maybe on Wednesday?" Kimmy asked.

Joy turned to me. "Kimmy's going through a very precise phase right now."Then she turned to Kimmy."I'll let you know when I think he's ready, okay? Remember how you didn't feel like talking much when you first got here?"

Kimmy nodded and then chewed on a piece of bacon.

"Anyhow, Devon, when you've had enough to eat we should get going," Joy said as she started to clear the dishes.Ted got up to help."You go ahead and I'll do these," he said.

She leaned over to kiss him on the cheek and I looked away. She wasn't gushy the way Lily had been with Dad, but it made me feel uncomfortable anyway.

* * *

As I expected, meeting the doctor was a nightmare. I hated sitting through his examination, especially since he already knew so much about what happened to me. I hated the way he looked at me and the uncomfortable questions he asked. His nervousness made me feel worse and it seemed pointless because I'd been through it already in Vietnam. The rest of the afternoon wasn't much better.The hour I spent with the social worker back at Joy's house dragged so slowly I thought I was going to lose it. I could barely even make myself say goodbye when she got up to leave. When she finally *did* leave the house, I couldn't stand another minute of being cooped up, and even though it was snowing, I decided to go for a walk. Joy found me in the entrance, pulling on the winter coat Detective Pearson had given me on the plane.

"Where're you going?" she asked.

"For a walk. Down to the docks."

She looked as if she was about to speak, but then she stopped herself. She scratched the side of her neck and I wondered if I was supposed to ask permission to go out. My friends always had to tell their parents where they were going, but Dad was different. His rules had been more relaxed.

"Do you think you should go alone?"Joy asked.

"I dunno," I said hesitantly, not knowing how I was supposed to answer.

"Maybe I should come with you?"

"I've done it hundreds of times. I know the way."

"I'm not concerned about you getting lost. I'm concerned about ... about ... well, someone recognizing you."

I looked down at my feet.

"It's just that nobody knows you're back yet," she said quickly. "The last thing in the news was that you'd been spotted in Cambodia and the police were investigating. As soon as someone sees you, they'll alert the media."

"But I can't stay inside for the rest of my life."

"That's true. I just think it might be good if someone goes out with you for the first couple of weeks – until interest in you settles down. It's going to be a bit crazy to start. But it will calm down eventually and then you can get back to normal."

"I thought they were going to have a press conference or something."

"It's scheduled for tomorrow morning. Detective Pearson called before breakfast to tell us. I didn't want to bombard you after everything you had to do this morning. Listen, I'm not saying you shouldn't go out. I just think it would be better if I came along. Do you mind? Ted can watch Kimmy, and I'd like to get some fresh air. I love the snow."

"If you want," I agreed finally and stepped outside.

I walked with my hood up and my face down. My fingers started twitching inside my pockets when we reached the main street and I had to pull them into fists to keep them still. I wasn't ready to be the center of attention or to see any of my old neighbors or classmates. Even though I'd thought about Vic a lot since leaving Vietnam, I wasn't even ready to talk to him yet. Joy walked beside me and held up her end of the silence. I glanced at the familiar storefronts and realized that nothing had changed since I left, not even the signs out front. It seemed wrong that so much could stay the same when I felt so different – when my life was crumbling to pieces, when Dad was gone.

I took us past the library, then past our townhouse. It was decorated with lights and a plastic snowman sat smiling in the front yard like a lie. I didn't linger, in case someone came outside and noticed us standing there, but as I walked away tears rushed to my eyes. I turned from Joy so she wouldn't see me wiping my cheeks. I remembered leaving in the dark that last morning and getting into the back of the taxi with Dad. We both thought we were going to save his life. Only Lily had known the truth.

Once we got to the docks, I pulled down my hood. I let the snowflakes land in my hair. There was nobody around so I felt safe showing my face to the crisp winter wind.

"Do I have to go to that press conference tomorrow?" I asked Joy.

"You don't have to do anything you don't want to do, especially where the media is concerned. Detective Pearson thinks it would help if you came because people want to see with their own eyes that you're okay. And then the curiosity would be over. But you don't have to go if you don't want to."

Joy was standing beside me, but she had her back to the wind. She had a scarf wound around her neck and a blue hat pulled down over her ears. Snowflakes covered her shoulders.

"If I *do* go, will I have to say anything?" I asked.

"You won't have to say anything or stay long. He'll read the same statement whether you stand beside him or not."

"When do I have to make up my mind?"

"Not until you get there. It's absolutely your decision."

"I'll think about it."

Waves slapped against the sides of the boats and flags flapped violently. I thought about Minh, An, Hien, and especially about Tham, and I wondered if they were still at the safe house. I knew it had only been a few days since I left, but it seemed much longer. I tried to imagine Minh's homecoming and hoped again that An would decide to go home too. I was sure none of them were facing a press conference, but I knew they faced their own challenges, probably worse than mine. Then I wondered if Tham would ever find a place to live and people like Joy and Ted who would care for her.

"What makes you to take in foster kids, anyway?" I asked Joy suddenly.

She was startled by my question and fumbled before she answered.

"It ... uh ... feels good to help. I like to think I'm making a difference. That maybe the kids we help – kids like you and Kimmy – will grow up and remember their time with us. That being with us, even for a little while, will help you get through some of the tougher times."

Her hands were punched down into her coat pockets and I could tell she was freezing.

"Isn't Kimmy staying?"

"There's a good chance Kimmy will go back to her mother."

"And you don't want her to?"

"I get pretty attached to the kids who come through our house. I hate to see them go. But I want what's best for them too. Most times that means going back home when everyone is ready."

"When I was ... away ... all I thought about was getting home. I thought

I'd get back and everything would be so easy. But it's not. And I don't think it's ever going to be the same. Now I don't know what I want. I don't even know what I'm supposed to want."

"It's going to be hard for a while. Getting back to school and seeing your friends, all of that. But therapy will help and we'll help the best we can. I bet some of your teachers will even be there if you need them. Then one day you'll realize you've slipped back into a routine and that some of the hard stuff has gotten easier."

I thought about what Joy said, but I didn't believe any of it. I didn't believe anyone could really help me or that anything would get easier. When I looked forward I couldn't see a thing – it was like looking into a deep, dark train tunnel, and it scared the hell out of me.

The cold wind made me shiver. I knew Joy would be happy to get walking again, so without another word, I turned away from the dock and pulled up my hood. I realized things hadn't changed so much after all. I still didn't have my own life, and in a way I was still trapped.

CHAPTER 34

The front page of the next day's newspaper freaked me out completely. It showed a picture of me and Joy walking down the street. Underneath the photo was a headline that said "Devon Sighting: Police Confirm Boy Home Safely." When I turned on the TV the story was on every channel and it was on the radio too. The newscasts were brief, but they were full of lies. They accused the police of covering up a kidnapping ring, of sneaking me back into the country to cover their butts, of inventing the whole story about Cambodia because they had bungled the investigation from day one.

I paced in front of the TV and flicked from channel to channel.

"Why are they saying those things?" I shouted in disbelief.

Joy came into the living room when she heard me and sat down on the rocking chair.

"Well, they have to report *something*, and if they don't know, they make it up." She pushed her feet hard against the floor until she was rocking quickly. The soft lines on her face had hardened.

We stayed together in the living room that way, pacing, rocking and switching channels, until Detective Pearson arrived an hour later. When he stepped up on the front porch, I ripped open the door and pulled him inside.

"Look at this! Listen to what they're saying. It's all a big lie. They haven't said a thing about Lily. It's all her fault and they're blaming you!" I kicked a cushion that had fallen on the floor.

"That's why we're holding the press conference, to help clear things up," Detective Pearson said.

"Aren't there laws against lying on TV?"

"It's all about freedom of speech, I guess," Joy said.

143

"We can talk about it some more on the ride over if you'd like," Detective Pearson said as he checked his watch. "But we should get going now or we'll be late."

We put on our coats and boots and got into Detective Pearson's car. When we started driving, my anger turned to fear and I found I didn't have anything more to say after all. I just sat silently and watched out the window. Even from two blocks away we could tell the press conference was going to be huge because there wasn't a single parking spot in sight. Detective Pearson whistled when he saw how many TV vans were lined up outside of police headquarters.

"It's going to be nuts in there," he said. "Are you sure you want to say something?"

"If it means putting an end to all of this crap," I said, feeling suddenly brave, "then yes."

"Just remember, you can change your mind at any time," Joy said.

I nodded and drummed my fingers on the car door.

Detective Pearson drove into an underground parking lot without any of the reporters spotting us. He explained exactly how the next hour was going to go.

"The Chief of Police is going to get up and read a statement about how we found you and got you home. He's going to thank the organizations and countries involved, then you and I are going to walk out on stage. I'm going to read this very short statement about my involvement and about how you're doing, then I'll ask if you have anything you'd like to say. If you do speak, don't go into any detail or mention any names. But if you want to say something about how it's good to be home and that you're feeling okay, then that's fine. We have a statement prepared for you, if it helps."

He handed me a type-written card.

"Then we'll get off stage while the Chief answers questions. In the meantime, we'll scoot down here, get back in the car, and get you home before anyone knows we've left the building. You can be back home watching TV again in an hour. Do you have any questions?"

I shook my head, and Joy reached over to squeeze my hand. We both had sweaty palms.

Detective Pearson checked his watch again.

"We have ten minutes. Joy, you can stay at the back of the stage when we go up. But stay right beside him the rest of the time. And don't be shy if the reporters start to crowd us. Push back if they get too close."

Joy nodded and I glanced at her anxiously. I couldn't imagine someone her size keeping back a crowd of reporters.

"Okay, it's time," Detective Pearson said finally and we climbed out of the car.

He took my arm and we walked quickly up a back set of stairs. Joy stayed glued to my other side. At the top of the stairs, we stepped into a small space behind a black curtain. He pulled it back so I could see that a stage had been set up in the front lobby. On the stage there was a podium, a microphone, and along the front, a row of potted flowers. Beyond the stage there were rows of chairs packed with people. Cameras were set up in a semi-circle around the stage and another row of people stood behind them. There was a steady flashing as the Chief of Police spoke, and I was so mesmerized watching it all that I didn't realize it was time to go on until Detective Pearson pulled gently on my arm.

We stepped across the stage to the microphone and Detective Pearson spoke while the room exploded with camera flashes. I stayed close to him, but the light still bounced into my eyes, and I had to blink back the brightness. My name was being yelled from all directions.

"Devon, what's it feel like to be home?"

"Devon, what happened to you in Vietnam?"

"Devon, did they hurt you in Vietnam?"

"Devon, how did you end up in Cambodia?"

"Devon, is it true that you were kept captive?"

"Devon, when do you think you'll go back to school?"

"Devon, what do you want to say to your captors?"

I could feel the sweat pooling in my armpits, and the floor felt as if it was moving under my feet. Even though the ceilings in the lobby were high, I felt them closing in. Then Detective Pearson looked at me and asked if I'd like to say a few words. I leaned toward the microphone and the room fell silent. For a brief moment the cameras stopped flashing. I looked down at my statement and the words were blurred. I looked back up and blinked. I struggled to open my mouth. I couldn't believe so many people cared what I had to say. Finally the words made it over my tongue.

"It's ah ... really, um ... great to be home. Thanks."

Then the cameras burst to life again and I felt Detective Pearson tugging on my arm. I stumbled off the stage and down the staircase into the police car. Joy and I ducked down in the back seat so nobody could spot us. It took ten blocks before my heart stopped pounding and I could breathe normally again.

"You did a terrific job," Detective Pearson said when we were almost home and sitting up again.

"Did I even say anything?" I asked.

"Yes. You were very composed."

"I doubt that."

"You can see for yourself very soon. I guarantee it will be on every newscast across the world tonight."

CHAPTER 35

After the press conference I felt as if I'd developed ADD or something. Nothing held my attention. I tried to watch TV, but I got tired of seeing my picture on news updates. I tried playing X-Box, but my fingers wouldn't work right and I got frustrated crashing on levels I'd beaten when I was eleven. At one point I even I punched my bedroom wall and split open my knuckles. Then I felt stupid and went to the study to check my email on Ted's computer.

The study was off the kitchen and it was full of books and papers scattered around the computer and printer. It was just a little room with a window that overlooked the backyard. On my first day, Ted had showed me how to use the computer. He explained about the filters he'd installed and how he'd be able to track what I was doing. He said it was for my own safety, but I think they were worried I'd Google myself and see stuff that would upset me more. As usual there wasn't anything but junk mail. That's all I'd had since I'd renewed my email and IM accounts and I'd already read everything Vic and Cody sent in the weeks right after I went to Vietnam. But I still hoped to hear from Minh or Tham. When my inbox turned up empty, I got up and started pacing again, like the tigers we used to watch at the zoo.

"What do you want to do, Devon?" Joy asked when she heard me back in the study.

I shrugged. "If I knew, I'd be doing it."

"Oh my God! You're bleeding!" she said when she looked down and saw my hand.

I licked my bloody knuckle and hid my hand.

"It's nothing. But I hit the wall and it's not so good."

"Can I see?" she asked.

I pulled out my hand and she looked close.

"It's not too bad. Let me get some ointment and a bandage."

She didn't say anything about the wall when she got back, but she continued talking as if nothing weird had happened.

"So do you want to get out of the house?"

"No. I don't want anyone to see me. I don't want to, like, make a big scene."

"Maybe we could go for a drive? At least you'd have a change of scenery."

I was about to agree when the phone rang. Joy stuck down the bandage and went to answer. But within a minute she said "no thank you" and hung up. The color had drained from her face.

"Who was that?" I asked.

"A TV talk show."

"What did they want?"

"You."

"Me? What for?" I asked. I had no idea why a TV show would be interested in me.

"To be a guest on their show."

"How did they find me here?"

"I have no idea," she said as she closed the curtains.

After that, the phone didn't stop ringing all week. Every TV talk show in America wanted to interview me and offered me money. Children's charities wanted me to be a spokesperson. Reporters and vans filled the street in front of our house.

When Kimmy went to peer out the window at all the commotion one day, afraid that Santa wouldn't get through, the cameras started flashing.

"Are you a movie star?" she later asked me suspiciously.

"No."

"Are you a famous football player?"

"No."

"Baseball?"

"No."

"Why are you so important then?"

"I haven't a clue."

Although I'd managed to get a few hours sleep each night before the press conference, the feeling of being captive again gave me nightmares. I woke up more than once crying from a dream where Minh, An, and Hien were still in the room under the kitchen and Long was punishing them for my escape. When I sat up after the worst one, my breathing was ragged and my chest was killing me. I reminded myself that the others were safe too – that Long was in jail. Still, the walls of my room felt uncomfortably close, so I got up and went downstairs. I turned on the living room lights.

"Can't sleep?" Joy asked from the top of the stairs. She was wearing a bathrobe and looked older without any make-up.

"No."

She came down and peeked out the window.

"Any reporters?" I asked.

"Looks clear, actually. First time in a week. It'd be a good time to take a walk." She smiled.

"I'm sorry for messing up your lives," I said.

"You're not messing up anything! And don't worry, we knew what we were getting ourselves into. Those reporters will disappear in another week or two. When something else happens, they'll race across the city to hound the next person who's caught their interest. Don't feel bad. Just concentrate on getting better," Joy said.

I had to stop to think – to try to remember what I used to feel like before everything happened.

"You probably doubt you'll ever be happy again," she said.

It wasn't the first time she'd read my mind.

"I dunno. Do you think I'm nuts?"

"No, I don't think you're nuts at all. In fact, I'm positive you're not. But you've been through a lot and it takes time to recover – time and therapy."

"Do you think I'll ever get over these dumb panic attacks?" I asked. The last thing I wanted was to freak out at school, or worse, black out and crash to the ground in a bathroom stall. Just thinking about such a small space frightened me. When I used the bathroom, I left the door open and whistled to let everyone know I was inside. I already knew there were certain smells, sounds, and sights – even just the sight of the basement door – that could set me off.

"I think you're already getting better. The breathing techniques are helping, aren't they?"

"I guess. I mean, I'm learning how to cope, but my attacks seem to be getting worse, too."

"I know sometimes it feels like you're going backwards, but soon you'll see you're making progress. You've got a lot of stuff locked away in your head, and it takes time for all of that to get processed."

"The thing is, I don't think I can keep going like this. All I do is hang out here every day and feel angry."

"Do you think you might be ready to see some of your friends? Was there someone you were particularly close to? I remember hearing about a friend of yours - Victor, maybe? He was interviewed on the news and he seemed pretty concerned about you. Maybe it's time to start making some connections to your old life again. Maybe that will help to relieve some of your anxiety."

I thought about Vic and tried to imagine what it would be like to see him again. I wondered if he'd be all weirded out around me, if he'd even want to see me. I knew I couldn't stand it if he looked at me strangely or if he couldn't look at me at all. But I also knew that seeing Vic would be the ultimate test. If things could be normal with Vic, then there was a chance I could get some of my old life back.

CHAPTER 30

I made my decision as soon as I woke up the next morning. I made a pact with myself in the bathroom mirror while I brushed my teeth: before the day was over I'd email Vic. I spent the rest of the morning putting it off. I cleaned my room and did the breakfast dishes. I beat an old high score on X-Box and played a game of Monopoly with Kimmy. I checked my email account twice, but as usual there was nothing new in my inbox. I finally dared to log onto a website my therapist had suggested – a website for survivors of human trafficking – even though I thought it would be creepy. Still, I couldn't forget about emailing Vic.

"You're a bit on edge," Joy said over lunch when the phone rang and I jumped in my chair. "Are you okay?"

"Yeah, it's just that I decided I was going to email Vic today." I said the words in a rush, as if saying them out loud would make me have to do it.

"That's great!" Joy said "And you know, you can always use the phone too if you want to call him."

"I thought it would be better to email first."

"Well, the computer's free," she said, then she watched me so long I felt as if I didn't have a choice but to finish my soup and go back to the study.

When I sat down at the desk I stared at the screen for twenty minutes before I could convince my fingers to type. I finally logged onto my email, but then I typed Vic's e-mail address in wrong and had to do it again. I agonized over what to write. I wasn't sure how much to say or how little. I wasn't sure if he'd be happy to hear from me or angry or freaked out. I tried to imagine I was him and how I'd feel, what I'd want to hear from me. In the end I wrote: *Hey Vic, Its me Devon. How RU?* Then I counted "Mississippis" while I got up enough courage to hit send.

I was still sitting at the computer when an instant message popped up on my screen.

Holy crap Devon is it really U?

Yup its me. I wrote back.

Seconds later another IM appeared.

I cant believe U finally wrote. R U OK?

Yeah Im OK

I saw U on the news, but didnt know where to find U. You didnt return my emails and then it said your account was shut down. I thought maybe U forgot about me

Im here I didn't forget

Where R U?

Near the school on Royal Amber Street.

Who R U living with?

Foster family theyre nice.

How long have U been there?

Since B4 Xmas.

U were there 4 Xmas?

Yup

How was it?

OK. Yours?

We got a Wii

Whats it like?

Good once U get used to it. We got baseball. U really get to swing the bat and pitch.

R U any good?

Better than in real life. Do you want to come over and try? Im just hanging out. Mom will be happy to see U 2.

Maybe. I have to ask.

OK. Go ask. I'll W8

I walked through the kitchen and found Joy in the living room.

"Vic wants to know if I can go to his house and play Wii." I was glad when she didn't look up and act happy.

"Would you like that or would you rather he came over here?"

I stopped and considered both possibilities.

"I think I'd like it better if he came over here. If he's allowed."

"That's no problem. Why don't you invite him over this afternoon."

I went back to the computer and typed.

Can U come here instead?

I hit send and then waited. I tried to keep my heart from bouncing right out of my chest. Finally his reply appeared.

Mom can bring me after lunch. How bout 1?

C U then. 745 Royal Amber.

The hour wait was unbearable. The minutes ticked by slowly and as one o'clock approached I was sure I was going to hurl. I paced around my bedroom and fidgeted like crazy, then I went down to the study and logged back onto the human trafficking website. I read some of what people had posted on the blog. It was hard to believe people could talk so easily about what they'd been through. I didn't think I'd ever be able to tell anyone other than the therapist what happened in Cambodia.

When the doorbell rang, I felt numb. It took a lot of effort to stand up. Joy met me in the entranceway.

"Do you want to do this on your own or have me hang around a bit?"

"Hang around a bit."

She was cool and stood in the background while I opened the door. Vic stepped in without saying a word and we both looked down at our feet instead of at each other. I scratched my arm and resisted the urge to run upstairs. When I stole a quick look at him I saw he was wearing a new winter coat and his hair was longer. The house became unbearably hot while I tried to think of what I should say. He must have felt it too because he unzipped his coat. Then, when he finally looked up, it happened. Our eyes locked and the weirdness between us melted. After a few seconds he looked exactly the same as he always had.

"Sorry I missed our birthdays ... and the big relay race," I said finally.

"We would have won if we'd had you, but this year we'll kick butt for sure."

"So what do you want to do?

"I dunno."

"Wanna play X-Box?" I asked.

"Sure," he said and kicked off his shoes.

Joy disappeared and I was glad not to have to make any introductions.

"Hey, I saw you in the newspaper," I said as we climbed the stairs.

"Yeah, I saw you in the newspaper too," he said.

Vic is the king of understatements.

CHAPTER 37

Three weeks after Christmas, Vic and Joy convinced me to go back to school. They didn't plan it together or anything, but they both said the same thing on the same day, and I had to admit they had a point. I couldn't spend the rest of my life going between the house and the therapist's office. I had to face the fact that I had a future, even though there were times when I wished I didn't.

Joy made arrangements with Mr. Morely, the principal, for us to come in after school on Friday afternoon to pick my classes for the winter term. We had an appointment at four, when everyone but the janitors would be gone for the weekend. As I walked with Joy down the sidewalk, I prayed I wouldn't see any of my classmates going home, even though I knew it was inevitable that I'd see them at some point. I don't know what I was expecting, but the school looked exactly the same, right down to the graffiti on the garbage cans by the sidewalk. Mr. Morely met us at the front doors.

"Devon, it's good to see you," he said. He was standing a little too straight and I could tell he felt uncomfortable.

I mumbled that it was good to be back, even though I didn't really mean it. I didn't look at him, but instead I looked at the trophy case and the lockers lining the halls. I'd forgotten the school had that gross smell of sweaty running shoes and floor cleaner. Mr. Morely introduced himself to Joy and made some lame comment about how happy all the kids and teachers would be to see me, that they'd all been worried when I didn't come back after two months. Then he led us to his office and asked us to sit down. Neither Joy or I said anything.

Mr. Morely rushed to fill the awkward silence. I wondered if all of the teachers would be as weirded out as he clearly was – if Mrs. Lamba would be able to teach math with me in the room, if Mr. Ahmed would look at me with pity. I dreaded looks of pity more than anything else.

"So, what classes would you like to try this term?"

He showed me the winter timetable and it was pretty easy to pick out my favorite teachers and subjects.

"I'd also like to have a special assembly to welcome you back," Mr. Morely said before we got up to leave. I thought he looked pretty happy with himself for coming up with the idea.

"I don't know about that," Joy said. She'd shifted to the edge of her chair as if she might jump up at any moment.

"I know it's a lot of pressure, but I think it might help things return to normal as quickly as possible – speed up the transition for Devon and the other students."

I imagined standing in the hall on my first day back while kids stared and whispered about me. I imagined walking into class and having the room go silent while the teacher stumbled on his words trying to find the right thing to say. Just imagining all the awkward moments made my palms sweat.

"But he's already had the press conference and so much attention in the media," Joy said hesitantly.

"Wait," I said quickly. "Maybe you're right. Maybe it *is* better to get it over with all at once."

Mr. Morley looked happy, but Joy scrunched up her face the way she did whenever something bothered her.

"Are you sure?" she asked me.

"I think so. I mean, I survived the press conference and now the reporters have lost interest. Maybe it will be the same here."

"Monday then?" Mr. Morely asked. "Just after the first bell? You can come along for support," he said to Joy.

"Only if we agree that Devon can back out if he wants," Joy said to Mr. Morely.

"Of course. He can cancel at any time," Mr. Morley said. His voice had dropped even lower than normal.

"We'll see you Monday, then," Joy said.

I could tell she still didn't like the idea.

CHAPTER 38

Sunday night was torture. I dreaded the assembly worse than the press conference because I knew I'd see my classmates and teachers – not just a bunch of strangers. I was so worried about what everyone would think that I couldn't stop tossing and turning. I couldn't stop imagining standing on stage and being stared at like a freak. I was afraid I'd do something to embarrass myself. When I finally did fall asleep, I dreamed about being trapped in Cambodia where I could hear Tham screaming in another room. I woke up exhausted, with a weight so heavy on my chest it was hard to breathe. I had to lay still and imagine my favorite moments with Dad when I was a little kid, the way the therapist told me to whenever I started to feel anxious.

Eventually I dragged myself up and got ready for school. I was like a zombie. I spent twenty minutes staring at my shirts before I could decide which one to wear. I couldn't find the toothpaste even though it was in my hand. When Joy offered me breakfast and some encouraging words, I ignored her.

Finally it was time to leave.

"I think we should walk," Joy said. "What do you think?"

"Whatever."

"The exercise might make you feel better."

"I already feel fantastic," I mumbled sarcastically.

"You don't have to do this if you don't want to. I can call Mr. Morely right now and cancel," she said.

I didn't answer. I just pulled on my coat and stuffed my feet into my boots.

Even though the temperature had dropped and the wind bit my

cheeks, I didn't zip up my jacket. Neither of us spoke while we walked, and I concentrated on keeping my mind blank. Eventually the school loomed at the end of the street and our arrival was a done deal. Mr. Morely welcomed us in the empty hallway, then lead us to the auditorium. My stomach churned. I'd never seen the school so still.

Joy and I waited backstage and listened to the shuffling bodies out front. My heart pounded above the sound of the introduction and I missed it all, except for something about "welcoming Devon home and being lucky to have him back and being a hero." The microphone screeched. Then the auditorium exploded with applause, and the principal motioned for me to join him on stage. Joy nudged me gently. I stepped forward and smiled, then I waved briefly at the sea of faces. Everyone stood and cheered. I looked around and saw an enormous banner on the wall that read "Welcome Home Devon." Teachers were wiping their eyes and some of the girls in the front row were crying too.

The clapping and cheering went on and on and I started to feel nervous about what to do next. My palms started to itch and my forehead felt clammy. The tightness in my chest spread so rapidly that I couldn't catch my breath. Mr. Morely was beside me suddenly and leaning toward me.

"Are you okay, Devon?"

His voice was a distant echo.

I felt his hand on my shoulder and in the same moment I thought I saw Minh's face in the audience. A wave of memories crashed into me just before my body short-circuited and my brain went blank. The last thing I remembered was the impact of hitting the floor.

When I woke up and realized I'd passed out on stage in front of the entire school, I wished myself back to sleep. I was in the nurse's room, lying on the bed. I'd been there another time when I got hit in the eye with a badminton racket and Dad had to pick me up early. Joy was with me this time though, sitting quietly in the corner and taking up about half the space Dad did. I didn't move. I hoped she wouldn't notice that I'd woken up, but she was impossible to fool.

"Hey there. Feeling okay?"

"Considering I just made an idiot of myself in front of the entire school?" I mumbled.

"I'm really sorry," she said.

I turned my head to the wall.

"What happened up there?" she asked.

"I panicked."

"Was it the noise? The attention?"

"All of it."

She watched me and waited until everything spilled out. "I know what happened in Cambodia doesn't, like, make me who I am. I know it's over, and that they can't hurt me again, but I can't stop feeling like something bad's just around the corner."

"That's completely understandable. I know you've heard this a lot, but it's going to take time."

"But *how* much more time? I don't think I can stand anymore of this. I feel like everyone can see how creepy I am."

"Nobody thinks you're creepy. Did you see how happy your friends were to see you?"

"They aren't my friends."

"Not all of them, no. But some of them are your friends. Vic is your friend."

"Vic, yes. The others just want to gawk at me."

"I think they want the best for you."

"I think they look at me and imagine all the things that happened to me. It's hard to look at people when you know all the stuff they know about you. If only the freakin' papers didn't report every little thing."

"Maybe some kids think about it at first. But then they see your strength and it inspires them."

"I don't want to *inspire* anyone. I just want to blend in the way I used to."

"In a few weeks things will go back to normal. I promise."

"How can you be so sure?"

"Because I've been where you are."

"What?"

"Ask anyone over fifty if they remember the Brechin case and they'll be able to tell you about it in gory detail. And yet nobody recognizes me on the street these days. Ever."

"What are you talking about?"

"The Brechin case. It was huge thirty-five years ago. I was fifteen when my younger brother and I were taken from our parents. The arrest afterward was sensational, the trial a media frenzy. Our faces were all over the papers and news for months. When I was finally ready to face the world, I couldn't go anywhere without being recognized. But it settled down eventually. And it will for you too, I promise."

I lay quietly as I thought about what Joy had just said. Finally I knew why she was so understanding and how she knew what I was feeling all the time. I'd never met anyone like her before – not even Dad could read my mind so well. I wondered if maybe Dad had been right all along and I did need a mother.

CHAPTER 39

As usual, Joy knew what she was talking about and school did start to feel normal. After a few days of awkward moments with my classmates and teachers, things slipped into a routine and I was just Devon again. By the end of February, I was doing better with my therapy too. I mean, I could at least talk instead of spending the entire hour looking at the clock. I hadn't passed out since the assembly and I'd stopped snapping at Joy. Ted and I had even started going to the rec centre on Saturday afternoons to play pick-up basketball, and it felt good to be doing something active again. Then, on one of those warm days at the end of winter, when people walk outside with their jackets hanging open and their heads and hands bare, my life took an unexpected turn.

. My day at school had been okay and I was heading home when I heard a woman's voice call out my name. I looked back at the front doors of the school, thinking it was a teacher or maybe the academic counselor again, maybe one of the secretaries from the office – but I couldn't see anyone. I heard it again, my name being called out, as if it was a question. I looked toward the front gates where kids were hanging out on the sidewalk and cars were parked along the street. Then I noticed a lady standing by the fence, clasping her gloved hands together, as if she hadn't noticed the day was so warm. I watched as she crossed onto the school property and stepped hesitantly in my direction. She was thin and fair and very freckled. She was dressed in blue jeans and a long winter jacket. There was a strained look in her eyes. But she didn't seem dangerous at all. I assumed she was the mother of a friend or someone who recognized me from TV.

"Devon?" she asked again. "I'm sorry to catch you like this out of the blue. But I was hoping I could talk to you for a bit?'

"Are you a reporter?"

"No, definitely not. But look, it's a bit more than a sidewalk conversation. Can we go somewhere for a coffee or a Coke?"

I stepped back and she reached out with her hands as if she was calming a nervous dog.

"Can we go across the street to the donut shop? We can sit in the window where everyone can see us. It's important."

The tone in her voice was so desperate it pulled me a step toward her. Then she started across the street and I followed. Before I knew it, I was sitting in the donut shop looking across a table at her.

"Would you like something to eat or drink?" she asked.

"No."

"How about a donut?"

"No, I'm fine."

She got up and went to the counter anyway, then returned moments later with a tray.

"I got you a Coke and donut, just in case you change your mind. Do you like the custard ones?"

I swallowed hard and told myself it was just a coincidence, that lots of people liked custard-filled donuts, not just me and Dad.

"I hope I haven't scared you. I mean, I didn't know how else to talk to you."

She fiddled with her coffee cup and I stared at her without touching my Coke or donut. There was something vaguely familiar about her face, but I couldn't figure out why.

"How are you doing at school?"

"You're not a reporter?" I asked again.

"No, nothing like that," she said.

"Then why are you asking me questions? Who are you and what do you want?"

"I have something important to tell you."

"Like what?" I asked impatiently.

She looked at me and I saw her eyes filling with tears.

"I promised myself I wouldn't cry," she said quietly and wiped her eyes.

"What do you want?" I repeated, more loudly this time.

An old couple at the next table looked over at us.

"Well, okay, here it is. The thing is, well, I'm just going to come out and say it."

She paused.

"I've got to get home or my foster mother will worry," I said as I pulled my backpack up from the floor.

"No wait, I have to say it. I just have to come out and say it." She took a deep breath and exhaled loudly. "I'm your mother. I know you probably find that hard to believe and if you *do* believe me I know you probably hate me, but I had to find you and explain."

I laughed and shook my head. I had no idea who this lady was or what she was trying to pull, but I wasn't buying her story at all.

"You *are* a reporter, aren't you? Or some type of con artist?"

"No, I swear, I'm your mother. It's true."

"Really? My mother?" I said with mock surprise. "Now that *is* a shock, especially since my mother's dead."

At that point I stood up, but she put her hand on my arm and her voice dropped to a whisper.

"Is that what he told you? That I was dead?" She paused and looked out the window, shaking her head. "Well, that's something I hadn't considered. But it would make it easier to explain, I suppose," she said

She sounded almost amused and a little bit hurt. She started digging in her purse.

"Look here. Please, just sit down for a few more minutes and look at these pictures."

She pulled out an envelope and laid down a series of photographs like a game of cards. They were my school pictures from Kindergarten up until Grade Six. At the end she laid down a picture of a man sitting on a couch holding a baby. They were both smiling at the camera. A woman sat on the couch too, watching the baby instead of the camera.

I sat down again and picked up the last picture. I studied it closely. There was no mistaking it was a picture of Dad, years younger, and that the baby was a redhead – just like the young woman in the photo, a younger version of the lady sitting across from me. I looked up at her. She was touching my school photos, shifting them frontward and backward with her fingertips.

"Your dad sent me a letter every Christmas with your school picture, just to keep me up-to-date. He told me what you were doing and what you were interested in. He sent some of your artwork too. I still have your Spiderman pictures on the wall. Well, to be truthful, he didn't send them to me, but to my mother – your grandmother. But we didn't get our Christmas picture last year, not the one just passed, but the one before that. I had no idea what happened until I saw you in the news last summer."

Her voice caught in her throat and she struggled to get it back.

"Sheila McIntyre?" It was all I could manage to say.

She smiled, wiped her eyes and nodded. "So you *have* heard of me?"

"Just your name."

"I'm not McIntyre anymore. I married three years ago. I wanted to see you before this, but your dad never included a forwarding address. And he must have started using a different last name sometime after you left. He must have been afraid I'd try to find you and that I wouldn't be, well, clean. Did he mention that I used to have an addiction problem?"

I nodded and stared at her. I knew she was telling the truth because Dad and I *did* have two last names. There was the last name on our official documents, like our passports, and the last name I used at school. When I asked him why one day, when I finally saw my birth certificate, he said it was because one had been his father's last name and one was his stepfather's last name – that he'd used both over the years. His story made sense and I never questioned him again. But even though I knew in that moment she really was my mother, I couldn't feel anything but anger and hatred toward her. It bubbled up inside me until I couldn't speak.

"I've been clean five years now," she continued. "I'm married and we have a house. And a baby boy. I'm so relieved that I found you finally. I've been so ... so ... tormented since you went missing."

My head started to spin and I knew I had to get into the fresh air or I'd collapse. Desperate, I jumped up from the table and knocked my Coke into her lap.

"I'm glad to know you've been living your happy little life while I've been through hell and back," I spat out, then walked from the restaurant.

When I got outside, I pulled my hood up. Then I headed for home, walking as fast as I could. I didn't slow down for anything, not even to cross the side streets. I dodged people on the sidewalk and accidentally knocked a purse from a lady's arm.

"Watch where you're going," someone yelled at me.

I didn't respond. I only looked back to be sure my mother wasn't following me.

CHAPTER 40

Joy and Kimmy were in the front yard when I came barreling up the driveway. They both looked up to say hi but I kept going. I didn't stop, even when Joy called out after me. I jumped up the porch stairs, burst through the door, and ran through the house with my boots on. I ran straight to my bedroom and slammed the door so hard I heard the wood splinter. I threw myself on my bed.

I heard a knocking a few minutes later.

"Devon? Are you okay?" Joy asked.

"Yes!" I shouted at the door.

"You don't sound okay. I'm worried. Can you tell me what's going on?"

I thumped my pillow with my fist and wanted to punch the wall, but I'd learned that lesson the hard way. Ted had left the hole in the drywall as a reminder, so I wouldn't split open my knuckles again, the way I had after the press conference.

She didn't say anything more and eventually my anger died down. When I opened the door, she was still waiting. I hung my head, afraid of what I might see in her eyes if I looked up.

"So, what's up?" she said in her softest voice – the one that could make me talk, even when I was determined not to.

"If you really must know, it turns out my mom isn't dead after all. She came and met me after school." I looked up to see her reaction and she raised her eyebrows. "The real one," I continued. "She even had pictures of us together when I was a baby."

Joy followed as I stepped back and sank onto my bed.

"Are you absolutely sure?"

I nodded.

"It turns out Dad had been sending her pictures of me every year – but no return address. And he changed our last name, she said, because he was probably afraid of her finding us. But she's clean now, apparently, and she's married with a kid."

"I'm not even sure what to say ... what did you say to her?"

"I don't remember. I was so angry I came home."

"Who are you most angry with?"

"Both of them. Her and Dad. I mean, they left me to rot in a hell hole!"

"But that wasn't their choice ... or their fault."

"If Dad hadn't kept her a secret, then I wouldn't have had to go to Vietnam in the first place. And if she hadn't been such a loser drug addict, Dad wouldn't have had to try to find me a stepmother."

"You know it never pays to play the 'what if' game."

"It's not a game. It's my life. And now it's a complete write-off."

Joy paused and I knew she wasn't willing to touch that topic.

"Don't you even want to find out more about her?"

"No."

"Maybe just give it a few days. Maybe you'll want to call and talk to her after you've had time to absorb this."

"I can't."

"Can't what?"

"I can't call her. I didn't get her number."

"I'm sure you can look it up."

"She's remarried. All I know is that she used to be called Sheila McIntyre."

My stomach lurched when I said her name out loud. Suddenly I realized I'd been talking to *my mother*. After thinking she was dead all my life, my mother was actually alive! She had found me and I screwed it all up by yelling at her.

I didn't know who to hate more at that point, myself or her. As usual, Joy guessed what was going through my mind.

"Don't worry. She's not going to give up that easily now that she's found you. I'm sure she'll give you a few days to cool off and try again. I know that's what I'd do."

By then my mind had moved on to a new dilemma.

"I can't believe Dad lied to me all those years. He told me she was dead," I said. "Why would he do that?"

"I don't know," Joy said, trying hard to keep up.

"I mean, he was always saying we had to be honest with each other. That it was the most important thing because there was only the two of us. Now I find out he was lying all that time. Why did he want to keep that from me?"

CHAPTER 41

I spent the rest of the night trying to figure out why Dad had lied to me. I didn't fall asleep until after two in the morning and even then I was restless. I woke up groggy and irritable and went through my day feeling miserable.

"What's up with you, anyway?" Vic asked me at lunch when he'd had enough of my one-word answers.

"Nothing," I said.

"Hey, you want to come over and play Wii after school? Eric and Cody are coming and we could play in teams. We got another remote."

"No. I just want to go home," I lied.

"What's the big rush?"

"Nothing," I said angrily. "I just feel like going home."

"Okay. Whatever. See ya later," he said and left the cafeteria.

After the final bell, I waited around the front of the school, looking for my mother. I stood talking to kids I wouldn't normally hang around with and stepped out of sight of Vic, Eric, and Cody when I saw them leave. When the sidewalk emptied, though, and the last kid hopped into the last waiting car, I walked home, angry at myself for missing the chance to go to Vic's and for fooling myself into thinking she'd be waiting for me again.

Of course I Googled her as soon as I got home, but nothing came up. I checked the online white pages and there was one S. McIntyre, but the address was for a super-fancy neighborhood and I was sure she didn't live there. I also checked on Facebook and MySpace, but still, there was nothing. I had no idea how else to try to find her, so all that week I waited after school, without admitting that I was looking for her. Instead, I told myself I was making an effort to get "involved" again, the way the therapist had suggested. I even convinced Vic to stand with me one afternoon to talk to some of the other guys from the track team, but my heart wasn't in it and he noticed.

"Why do you keep looking down the street?"

I shrugged.

"Are you waiting for someone?"

"No."

By the end of the second week I became even more short-tempered. I couldn't blame her for not coming back – I could only blame myself and make excuses for her. She must have a job, I reasoned. Maybe she can't always get afternoons off to talk to long-lost sons. Maybe she was sick. Eventually I told myself I hadn't lost anything because I'd never had her in my life in the first place. But it didn't make me feel any better. After the third week of waiting, I walked home with my head hanging as low as Homer Simpson's when he knows he's in deep trouble with Marge. As soon as I came through the door, Joy called to me from the kitchen.

"Devon? Can you come in here for a minute?"

Talking to Joy, or anyone for that matter, was the last thing I wanted to do, but I slumped into the kitchen and sat at the table. She put a snack in front of me.

"You've been coming home late the last couple of weeks. Have you joined an activity after school?"

I shook my head.

"Have you been staying for extra help with your schoolwork?"

Again I shook my head.

"Just hanging out with your friends?"

"Yeah, just hanging out."

"I think there's something more, and I was hoping you'd tell me what's going on."

I was too embarrassed to talk about it, but I watched her expression change as she figured it out.

"It's because she hasn't come back yet."

I stared at the table.

"But she will. She's just giving you time."

"Three weeks?" I asked and stood up.

I left my snack untouched and left the kitchen. I went up to my room. I didn't believe my mother was giving me time. I believed she was giving up on me. For once I knew Joy was wrong about something. I lay on my bed and looked up at the ceiling. It started to sink toward me and the walls closed in until I felt like I was in a coffin.

At that moment I hated everyone and everything. I hated my mother for leaving me for a bag of crack. I hated Dad for meeting Lily. My hate for Long and Lily filled every empty space inside me but left enough room for me to hate the men who hurt me in Cambodia, and to hate Minh, An, and Hien for knowing what I had been through. I hated my classmates and every person on the street who had stared at me with so much knowing in their eyes that I wanted to die rather than consider what they were thinking. I even hated thinking about wanting to die because I knew Joy was already worried about me and was on some sort of high alert – that she'd had the therapist prescribe some sort of pills, just in case I needed them. I even hated Joy and Ted for bothering with me at all. But more than anything, I hated myself.

CHAPTER 42

When I couldn't stand another minute of being closed up in my bedroom, I went downstairs to the computer. I checked to see if Vic was on Instant Messenger, but he wasn't, so I checked my email. There were two new messages. One had a subject line that read: *Want to chat with a lonely girl* that I deleted right away and a second one had a subject line that read: *To Devon From Tham*. I blinked twice, but it was still there. I didn't think it could be real, but I opened it anyway.

Hi Devon. It is me Tham. I learned to use the computer and send email. I hope you are there.

I read it ten times to convince myself it really was Tham writing then I wrote back quickly with my blood pumping loudly in my ears.

Tham. Is it really you? I can't believe you learned to use the computer so fast. What are you doing and where are you? Devon

I hit send and then felt empty. I sent another quick reply.

PS I hope you are okay.

I waited five minutes and checked my in-box again and again, but there was nothing new. I had to remind myself that with the time difference it would be hours before Tham would read my message. I also knew the next twenty-four hours were going to kill me, but even still, my shoulders felt lighter than they had in weeks.

The following day dragged at school. I went to the computer room at lunch to see if Tham had written yet, but she hadn't. I could barely concentrate on anything my teachers were saying. Instead of writing an outline for an essay in English as I was supposed to, I thought about Tham. I wondered, as I often did, about what she was doing and where she lived.

When the bell rang, I bolted from class and walked home so quickly I got a cramp in my side. I jumped over Kimmy's scooter on the driveway, slammed into the house, and kicked off my shoes. They landed next to a pair of boots I'd never seen before. But I didn't stop to question whose they might be. Instead I headed straight through the kitchen for the study. I stopped short, though, when I saw Joy sitting at the table with Kimmy and my mother. They were drinking tea and sharing a plate of Joy's special lemon loaf. I steadied myself against the doorframe.

"Devon!" Joy said brightly.

"Look who's here!" Kimmy said with eyes the size of full moons.

I grabbed a chair and sat down.

"I'm sorry I startled you last time," my mother said softly.

"I'm sorry I took off," I said. I could barely look at her face, but for once my brain cooperated and the words came out exactly the way I wanted them to.

"It's really ...all my fault," my mother stammered. "I shouldn't have ambushed you like that. I should have gone through children's services to contact you. But once I tracked you down, I just couldn't resist. I had to see for myself that you were *my* ... the same Devon."

I couldn't think of what to say but that was okay because she continued in a rush.

"Joy said you've been pretty upset that I didn't come back. And I'm sorry. I want so badly for this to work out for ...us."

I sneaked a look at Joy. She was smiling at me slightly and I realized my mother and I finally had a chance to make it right.

"The past has been ugly for both of us and that's my fault – I know," she said. "I wish I could change it, but I can't. I can only change the future and I swear, I'm not going to screw that up too."

She paused.

"I mean, look at me. I'm a complete stranger to you. You have every right to hate me. But I hope you won't when you get to know me. I mean, I guess what I'm trying to say is, I hope you'll *try* to get to know me. I'd like it very much if you'd come for dinner one night soon. My husband Brad can't wait to meet you, and I want you to meet your little brother."

Again I looked to Joy and she was still encouraging me with that smile of hers.

"Am I allowed?" I asked.

"Of course," Joy said. "We've been in touch with children's services and they're very supportive of you having regular visits."

"After I contacted them, to find out where you were living, they came over to interview us and inspect our house," my mother explained. "They did background checks and we passed. That's what's been taking so much time. Like I said, I had to do things right this time around. You don't have to answer today. You can think about it and let me know. I've written down our address and phone number. And look, I brought a picture of Mitchell and Brad."

She pushed a picture across the table to me. I picked it up and looked closely.

"Mitchell turns two in July," she offered.

"He has red hair," I said

"He looks a lot like you did at that age."

I threw her a questioning look.

"Yes, I was still with you then," she said quietly.

Mitchell was a cute kid with a big smile, and Brad looked like a nice-enough guy. He had the eyes of someone I could maybe even trust.

"It seems like just a few months ago you were learning to walk," she said. "I can't believe it's been twelve years. You were the best thing that happened to me. But your father was right to take you away."

"You're not angry at him?" I asked.

"Sometimes yes, sometimes no. Sometimes I don't know how to feel."

I nodded. I knew exactly what she meant and I liked that she didn't have an answer. It made me feel as if I wasn't so alone.

CHAPTER 43

After my mother left, I thought of twenty different questions I wished I'd asked. I wanted to know if she had any brothers or sisters, how she met dad, if she ever missed him the way I did. Even the next day I could think of nothing but all the things I didn't know about her and it was hard to hide the fact that I was distracted. I didn't even realize how zoned out I was until computer class when Vic elbowed me in the ribs.

"What?" I whispered.

He was busy opening my instruction book.

"What Vic is trying to point out," the teacher said as he walked toward us, "is that I just asked everyone to import the picture of their choice from the photo library into Photoshop."

I hurried to catch up and the teacher leaned over my desk. I could tell he wasn't really angry.

"If you find you're falling behind, don't be afraid to ask for help," he said.

I nodded and scrolled through the photo library.

"You've been, like, really out of it the last few weeks," Vic whispered. "I mean, well, *more* out of it than usual. What's up?"

"A lot of things actually. Like a girl I met in Cambodia emailed me."

"A girl?"

"Yeah, and I keep waiting for her to email again."

"Ohhhh," he said knowingly.

"It's not like that," I whispered.

"Whatever," he said and rolled his eyes.

"And there's something else ..."

"Like what?"

"Like I found out my mother's alive."

Vic glanced up at the teacher, then said to me, "Seriously?"

"Seriously. I met her yesterday. She tracked me down after all the crazy publicity."

"Where's she been?"

"She lives out in the east end with her husband and baby boy."

"You have a brother?"

"Yeah, heavy, huh?"

"Did your dad know?"

"Apparently."

"And he never said?"

I shook my head.

"That is heavy. Are you going to go live with her?"

"I dunno. We haven't even had dinner together yet. I'm supposed to call her when I decide I'm ready."

He stared at me as if it was a no-brainer and I should be on the phone with her already.

"What are you waiting for? Call her tonight."

"I will," I said. "When I get home from school."

Even before class ended, I closed my books. Then I was out the door and down the hall before Vic could stop me to ask more questions. When I got home, I went straight to the phone and dialed, even though my hands were shaking uncontrollably.

"Hi," I said when I heard my mother answer. "It's me, uh, Devon."

"Oh." Her voice broke and when I didn't hear anything else, I wondered if we'd been disconnected. Finally she cleared her throat.

"I'm so glad you called," she said. "I thought you'd need a few days to think things through. I mean, I told myself not to be disappointed if I didn't hear from you right away. So thank you ... for not making me wait."

"I hate waiting too," I said.

There was a pause.

"So do you want to come over for dinner?" she asked.

"Yeah."

"I have to work all weekend at the hospice downtown. I help with the cleaning and I try to keep the patients comfortable. What about Monday? I think I can wait two days if you can."

"I can wait."

"Then I'll pick you up at home after school?"

"Okay."

"What do you like to eat?"

"I dunno. Everything but rice. Surprise me."

When we hung up, I was so excited I practically bounced into the study to email Vic the good news. I logged on for a third time that day and, suddenly, there was a reply from Tham. She'd written and told me all about the English classes she was taking at night and about the job she had during the days at a vegetable market. She said she was living with a nice family and was applying for a study visa to come to America. Apparently her English teacher was American and was helping her with the application process. I read and reread her email. Then I wrote to her about Joy and Ted, and about meeting my mother. I asked her if she knew anything about Minh, Hien, or An. And since I knew she'd understand, I told her about the things I was struggling with too. It was a relief to be honest with someone who I *knew* would understand. When I hit send, a moment of loneliness washed over me, but then I remembered dinner with my mother on Monday.

With two big things to wait for, it was no wonder the weekend went by slowly. Even though Joy took me and Kimmy to the movies on Saturday night and I spent Sunday afternoon with Vic practicing nosegrinds at the skateboard park near his house, I didn't think the weekend would ever end.

It wasn't until after dinner on Sunday that I got a reply from Tham. Then I was psyched. She told me she'd read about me on the Internet and didn't understand why my case got so much attention when kids in Vietnam disappear all the time without much notice. She told me she understood what I was going through, but that I shouldn't feel ashamed. She said I should be happy like she was and I should enjoy being free finally. She hadn't seen any of the others, except An. She said he lived with a family too and was going to school – and that he was even smiling sometimes.

Before I wrote back, I thought hard about what Tham had written. I wondered why kids went missing in Vietnam and never made the news when my disappearance was such a huge deal. It didn't seem fair that so many people worked to find me but that the police in Vietnam had never even known to look for Minh, An, Hien, or any of the girls, and that they would still be locked in up it wasn't for me. I wondered how many other kids were suffering every day behind locked doors. I shuddered at the thought.

I wished suddenly that I could make it better for someone else, the way people were trying to make it better for me. That's when a switch flicked in my head – that's when I realized that *I* could make a difference for others if I could just fix myself first. That's when I knew I wanted to get my head together and I started to figure things out, just a little bit at a time.

CHAPTER 44

Just when I thought time had stopped moving, Monday afternoon arrived. I sat on the steps waiting for my mother while Joy swept the porch.

"Nervous?" she asked when I started to tap my foot.

"Yeah. I guess. I mean, it's hard not to be."

"I know. But I'm sure it'll go well."

"I hope so."

"Just try to relax," she said as she sat down next to me.

I did my best to smile.

The conversation died and we both sat in silence until a blue Echo pulled into the driveway. My mother climbed out and said to Joy, "I'll have him home by nine, if that's okay."

"That's fine," Joy said and waved. "Have a good time."

My mother opened the passenger door and I got in.

"Sorry about the mess. Mitchell thinks it's fun to throw Cheerios on the floor."

"That's okay," I said, glancing in the back seat.

"Brad and Mitchell went for pizza and won't be home until after dinner, so we have a bit of time to ourselves," she offered as we pulled out of the driveway.

I nodded, but I didn't say anything. I sat quietly and watched to see where we were going. As she drove, she glanced frequently in her rearview mirror, then over at me. After several blocks, she turned on the radio. It was a relief to have voices fill the car. We drove east, beyond our neighborhood and out onto the highway where the cars were speeding past.

"I hope we miss rush hour," she said.

"Me too," I said before I let the sound of the radio fill the car again.

When we left the highway we drove through an area of small bungalows. Each house had a small front yard, a small backyard, and a detached garage. There were large trees that were just starting to bud and the grass was turning green. When we pulled into a driveway and my mother turned off the car, I took a long breath and exhaled slowly, counting the seconds in my head.

"You okay?"

I nodded.

"How do you feel?"

"Scared."

"Me too," she said with relief.

The house inside was clean, but almost bare. The living room had only a couch, an armchair, and a box of toys.

"We moved here from a small apartment so we're still furnishing the place. But it works for now – it gives Mitchell lots of room to play."

She continued to show me around. The kitchen was small but tidy with a table pushed against one wall and a high chair in the corner. Mitchell's room was small, but it was packed full of things: toys, diapers, a crib, clothes. Finally she showed me the third bedroom at the end of the hall.

"This is your room," she said. When I looked confused she added, "For when you're ready to stay over sometimes."

We walked in and I recognized the smell of fresh paint. There was a bed, a desk, and a dresser set. There were books on a shelf, a skate-board leaned up against the wall, and two brand-new baseball gloves on the desk.

"We got you a few things so you'd feel at home. We weren't sure what you liked, but Joy helped us," she said and stepped inside, motioning for me to join her.

"Do you remember these?" she asked as she pointed to framed pictures on the wall. They were pictures I'd drawn when I was younger, and one, especially, I did remember drawing. Dad told me it was for my grandmother and I'd assumed he meant his mother, who'd lived in a nursing home at the time. I'd worked hard on it – I copied it from a picture in my Spiderman coloring book.

I looked around the room and I was struck suddenly with the image of my mother sitting in that room, waiting for me to visit, the same way Lily had fussed over Quan and Sang's rooms.

"Wow," was all I managed to say.

"Well, anyway, we had to guess at the colors and things, so I hope you'll feel comfortable."

She paused and when I didn't reply, she continued.

"Are you hungry?"

"Yeah, I guess."

"Do you like spaghetti and meatballs?"

I nodded and swallowed the lump in my throat.

"Good. Let's go eat."

I sat at the kitchen table while she pulled containers out of the fridge.

"I made it last night so I could just heat it up today. I didn't want to waste our time together cooking, and I always think pasta tastes better when it's reheated," she said as she scooped noodles and sauce onto a plate.

"That's what Dad used to say, too," I said, hoping it was okay to mention him.

"Yes, we did have that in common." She turned and smiled.

"What else did you have in common?" I asked.

"Oh, lots of things," she sighed. "We both liked baseball." She put a plate in the microwave and turned it on. "And I hear that you play too, right?"

"Yeah," I said.

"Good."

"What else did you have in common?"

"I dunno. Um, let's see. We both loved custard donuts, we both liked basketball."

"You play basketball?"

"Not now, but when I was young I did. I used to skateboard too."

"Really?"

"Until I broke my arm."

The microwave beeped and she took out the plate. She set it down carefully on the counter then put in another.

"Did you do any girl things?"

"Not so much," she said with a little laugh. "But I do now – like cook a fantastic spaghetti sauce. Here, eat up, " she said as she put a heaping plate in front of me.

I dug right in without waiting.

"It tastes just like Dad's," I said with my mouth half full.

"That's because I showed him my secret recipe."

After we ate dinner and did the dishes, she pulled out a photo album. She showed me pictures of my grandparents and of herself growing up. She showed me pictures of her and Dad when they were first dating. She showed me pictures of me as a baby with people I didn't recognize. She didn't offer a lot of explanations or try to hug me, but I could tell she wanted to.

"Brad will be home soon. Do you want to go out back and play catch? The ground's a little damp, but if we stay on the high part we should be okay," she said after we'd gone through all the photos.

"Can you throw?"

"A bit," she said and we went out to the backyard with the gloves from my room.

My mother had a good arm. She threw hard and straight. We threw back and forth in silence. The rhythm of the ball became our conversation. Sometimes it went gently between us and sometimes we threw it hard. Sometimes I missed a high ball and had to run to fetch it and throw it back.

Brad and Mitchell found us in the backyard just as it was starting to get dark. Mitchell was holding onto a Bionicle toy with one hand and Brad's pant leg with the other. When my mother introduced us, Brad shook my hand like a friend. Mitchell hid his face at first and peeked from behind Brad's leg. But eventually, by the end of the night when we were back in the living room, Mitchell brought me a toy truck.

"That's a good sign. He never shares his trucks," Brad said.

I thanked Mitchell for the truck and got down on the floor to play with him. Even though I had no experience playing with kids that little, I must have done okay because he brought me more cars and trucks, and before long, we were driving them all over the empty living room. I remembered playing cars with Dad when I was little, spending rainy Sundays building roads with Hot Wheels tracks and driving our cars all around a city we called Devonville.

Finally, my mother stood up from where she had been sitting, watching us.

"We better get you home," she said to me. Then to Mitchell she said, "Honey, it's time for Devon to go home, but he'll come back soon to play with you – won't you, Devon?"

I nodded and stood up. Mitchell ran over and handed me a toy truck – the red one I'd been driving.

"That's okay, Mitchell. You keep your truck." I tried to give the truck back, but he refused to take it.

"Nestime," he said and curled my fingers around it.

"Sure – I'll keep it safe and bring it back with me next time," I said and smiled.

CHAPTER 45

Joy was the one who brought up the idea that I could live with my mother and Brad. I'd been going for regular overnight visits by then and things were pretty good. Sure, I'd thought about it as a possibility, but in my mind it was something I might do in a year or two. Then Joy said I could move whenever I was ready.

"How will I know if I'm ready?" I asked.

It was early June, two weeks after my fourteenth birthday, and we were sitting on the front porch in shorts and T-shirts.

"Just imagine yourself living there and see how it feels."

I closed my eyes and tried to imagine living there full-time, dealing with Mitchell every day and having to get used to another set of parents.

"Scary," I said.

"Scarier than when you came to live with us?"

"No – that was different."

"Yes, but you managed all the bumps and it's pretty smooth going now, don't you think?"

"Yeah. Of course you're like a mind reader or something. You understand me."

"I bet your mother's pretty understanding too."

"Do you want me to go?"

"Of course not! You are always welcome here. I just want what's best for you – in the long run."

"And you think that's living with my mother?"

"Only if that's what you want."

"Do you think it's what she wants?"

"I'm positive."

"Did you talk to her about it?"

"Yes."

"And she said she wanted me to live with her?"

Joy nodded and I felt my cheeks burn. "If I *do* go, will you get another kid?"

Joy laughed. "Yes, we'll *get* another kid when one needs us."

"I'll have to think about it. It's a big decision. I haven't even figured out whether to call her Sheila or ...Mom."

"I'm sure she doesn't care much either way, as long as you're in her life."

Saying I'd think about it was an understatement. Once the idea was in my head, I couldn't *stop* thinking about it, about her. Instead of waiting until the weekend to tell her something, I started to call her whenever the idea popped into my head. She was always happy to hear my voice. One time I called at ten o'clock to tell her about the time Dad and I made the porcupine fish out of papier-mâché, about how it took us all night and the kitchen ended up looking like we'd had a food fight. She laughed and I could tell she wasn't just trying to be polite. It wasn't long before I realized what Joy had known all along – that I belonged with her and Mitchell. I even belonged with Brad. I belonged with my family.

Living with them meant moving across the city, but I was due to start high school in the fall anyway. Vic was bummed when I told him, but I promised we'd still see each other on weekends.

"I'll still be in the same city. I'm not leaving the country or anything," I explained.

"I know. But high school won't be the same without you."

"What about me? You'll still have Eric and Cody, and I'll have to make all new friends."

"That won't be hard – you're practically famous."

I frowned. I knew moving meant a lot of changes. I'd have to get used to a new family and a new neighborhood, and going to a new school meant another settling-in period when everyone realized who I was.

"Maybe by then, everyone will have forgotten about me," I suggested hopefully.

"So when are you moving?"

"Middle of July. I'll have you over as soon as I get unpacked," I said.

"This summer's really going to suck," he complained.

"No it won't. You can come over there and I can come here. It's going to be great. You'll see."

"If you say so," Vic said, determined to sulk.

* * *

Moving day was a bit like my last day in Vietnam. I was happy about going home but sad about leaving the people I cared about. Joy tried not to cry when I packed the last of my things into Brad's car. I tried not to cry either, but it was hard to say goodbye. I could see in her face how much she wanted me to be happy. She didn't say it, of course, but by then I was good at reading her mind too.

"I'll visit you guys all the time," I said as I hugged her. "I promised Vic I'd still be a regular in the neighborhood so I'll stop by and meet your new kids."

"You'd better," she said and wiped her eyes. "It's not fair saying goodbye to you and Kimmy so close together."

I went to shake Ted's hand but he wrapped his arms around me instead. "If you ever want someone to play basketball with, you know where to find me."

Brad closed the trunk and settled himself into the driver's seat while my mom and Joy had a few final words.

"You'd think I'd get used to this part, but I never do," Joy said through the car window as I buckled myself in next to Mitchell. "At least I still get to see you."

Joy and Ted stood in the driveway and waved as we drove away.

Even though I'd been many times to the east end of the city where Mom and Brad lived, even though I knew our house well by then, and even though I knew the neighborhood, I'd never before realized how close we were to the city zoo. But that day Brad took a different route, one that took us by the back entrance and down a side street past a tire shop.

"Did Dad know that you live out here?" I asked before my mind even finished putting the thought together.

"I don't think so. We moved here a few months before you went missing." The word *missing* still caught in her throat.

"What month did you move?" I asked.

"March."

"We were still here then," I said.

"What makes you ask?" Brad said, glancing in the rearview mirror at me.

I must have gone pale because he pulled the car to the side of the street and they both turned around to look at me.

"Devon? Are you okay?" he asked.

I didn't speak for a few moments, but I remembered clearly what my father had said in Vietnam in the days leading up to his death.

"Honey?" my mother said gently.

Even Mitchell stopped chattering and was looking at me with wide eyes.

"Dad only told me your name once. It was when he was dying. He told me he was going to call you to tell you what a good kid I was. He said you lived in the east end of the city, near the zoo and by a tire shop. I thought he was delirious. But he must have known where you lived."

"Maybe he did. Maybe he was in touch with Grandma and she told him."

"He must have known," I said, then I repeated it over and over again.

"Maybe he kept track of me after all. Maybe he was just waiting ... until he was sure I was ready," my mother suggested.

"I don't understand," I said. "I just don't understand."

While I shook my head and tried to fit the pieces together, Brad put the car into gear and drove us home.

After My Story Ended

It's weird, but Tham arrived in America the same day Lily was sent back to Vietnam. I often wonder if their planes crossed in the air. It was Detective Pearson who told me about Lily. He emails me whenever he has updates. He's also the one who told me about how Quan and Sang were fighting to stay in the country, even though they had fake passports.

One winter afternoon, after Tham had been in America for a few months, she said, "I thought you told me once that you wanted to help people – like you and me."

"Yeah, I do," I said.

"So, when?" she asked.

We were sitting in a coffee shop on her campus, not far from where she shared an apartment with five other students. She turned and hung her winter coat off the back of her chair.

"When what?" I asked.

"When are you going to start?"

"I dunno. When I'm grown up."

"You're already sixteen! Do you think you'll be more helpful when you're older?"

The thing that I've learned is that there's always someone in your life who makes you try harder, even when you think you're already doing your best. For me, that person is Tham.

"No. Probably not," I admitted.

"Then I think it's time."

"Do you have something in mind?" I asked. By then I'd spent enough time with her to know about her big master plan. She has all her life goals mapped out and every day she does some little thing toward one of them, even on bad days.

"Yes, actually. I think we should start volunteering at a shelter down the street. They rescue people who've been *trafficked*." She tripped over the word trafficked, but then recovered. "They find people who've been brought here and kept illegally, then help them get their lives started again."

"Are there really people in *this* city like that?" I asked. It didn't seem possible that what happened to us in Cambodia could be happening so close by.

"Of course there are! There are people all over the world who are lured with promises of work and then tricked into prostitution or terrible working conditions."

"So what do you want me to do?"

"They need volunteers for everything — from cooking to fundraising. But I think we should try to reach out to the people who stay there. I mean, I saw a girl there last week. I know she needs us, the way we needed the people who helped us at the safe house."

"But I'm not a social worker, or a therapist. What can I do?"

"You can show her that you understand. I think she needs to meet someone who's gotten through. Like you."

"Or you," I pointed out.

"Yes, or me. But I can't do it by myself."

I kept trying to protest. I complained about how long it took me to get downtown, how I was only just getting my head around things, that my nightmares weren't completely gone.

"But can you go down into a basement?" she asked.

"Yes," I said. "But that's different."

"No, it means you've gotten through." I started to protest again, but she held up her hand.

"Save it, Devon. I'm going this week to sign up as a volunteer. I think you should too."

There was no arguing with Tham, so that Wednesday I took the bus downtown to the shelter and we signed up for two afternoons a week. I was scared, but because I'd get to see Tham two more nights a week, it was a no-brainer.

We went through orientation one weekend then started our regular shifts. On my first afternoon at the shelter I saw her – Tham didn't even have to point her out. I knew which one she was, just by looking at her eyes. They looked sad the way Tham's eyes used to and when I saw her my heart fell suddenly, the way it does when you drop into your first half pipe on a new skateboard. I approached her slowly and sat next to her. She was looking out a window.

"Want to get out and go for a walk?" I asked.

"No. It's too cold," she said. She had sleepy blue eyes and wavy blond hair.

"Maybe another day then? When it's warmer? We could go down to the docks and see the ships."

She shrugged, turned, and went to sit on a couch. She picked up a magazine and started flipping through.

"So, do you like it here?" I asked, then cringed when I realized how stupid my question sounded.

"Would you?" she asked. "It's like jail."

"Oh. Is there somewhere else you'd rather be?"

"Back at work."

"Where do you work?"

"I was working at a Health Spa. But the police raided it and brought us all here. They said we were working illegally."

"Did you like that job?"

She kept looking out the window and didn't answer.

"How old are you?" I asked, trying another way to get her talking.

"Sixteen, next month," she said.

"How did you end up here?"

"I saw an ad in the paper. The money was good. I came so I could bring my parents over."

"Were you tricked?"

She turned her shoulder from me.

"I know sometimes people get forced into doing things they don't want to," I said.

"Oh yeah? What do you know?" she asked. Her tone was bitter but I knew she was really just trying to hide her shame.

I took a deep breath and forced myself not to chicken out.

"A lot more than I'd like to know."

She finally looked at me.

"Like what?" she challenged.

"Like what it feels like to be so ashamed you can barely breathe."

"Really? What's your name, anyway?" She had a rough edge, but I doubted it would last much longer with me.

"Devon. And yours?"

"Anna."

"Nice to meet you, Anna."

"I guess," she said.

"You know, the people here can help you stay in America. There's a law that protects people who've ended up working here ... against their will. It helps them stay and start a new life."

Anna went still and stared at the floor. Then she looked up slowly. Her eyes were blurry with tears. That's when I knew I had her attention, that we were going to make things better for her.

"I'd really like to tell you about how I got rescued. If you want to hear," I said quietly.

She nodded and wiped her eyes with the sleeve of her shirt.

* * *

It took weeks for me to unravel this story for Anna. Sometimes Tham sat with us and sometimes she helped in the kitchen or talked to the other people staying there – the young women mostly. But each afternoon Anna and I sat together by the window and somehow I found a way to be honest with her. She took it all pretty calmly, like someone who knows what it's like to be humiliated. In between me telling her this story, she told bits of hers. They are both sad stories, but the surprising thing was that sharing mine helped me as much as her. Since meeting Anna, I've told others this story too, mostly young people who arrive at the shelter and don't trust anyone, who think they're to blame for what's happened to them. I like telling them because it makes them open up and then we can help.

Another thing I started doing is what the shelter calls public outreach. Even though I thought I'd never get up on stage again, I sometimes talk to groups about how human trafficking happens everywhere in the world, even in America. I explain that it's sometimes hard to recognize when someone's being held against his or her will and why some people are afraid to tell the truth about what's happening to them. I give people signs to look for and the kinds of questions to ask. Tham never speaks publicly, but she always finds me new groups to talk to.

When I first got back to America I wished people would stop staring at me. I wanted people to look right through me. But now I like it when people look at me. When people do recognize me, it's usually because of my red hair. Then they wonder if I'm okay. Most people don't believe me when I say "life is good." If they dare to question me, I explain that, in the end, it was impossible not to be affected by all the great people around me, like Mitchell who gets excited about something as simple as going to the park, like my mother who's so grateful to have me around she still looks twice when I come out of my bedroom, or like Tham who's determined to make the world a safer place.

What I've come to realize is that happiness is my choice. I can choose to let the past ruin my life and nobody will ever blame me if I use it as an excuse to fail, or I can wake up every day and choose to be happy. Some days the choice isn't so easy. Panic still creeps in now and then and the memories suck big time, but I know they can't hurt me now. Most days, when I feel the sun on my face, I know I've been at the bottom and I'll never be there again. I know there are lots of people cheering me on and that there are lots of people who still need my help.

About the author:

Christina Kilbourne lives in Mount Albert, Ontario. She received her master of arts degree in creative writing and English literature from the University of Windsor. Her books include *Dear Jo: The story of losing Leah ... and searching for hope*; *The Roads of Go Home Lake* (BookLand Press); and *Where Lives Take Root* (BookLand Press). Visit Christina at www.christinakilbourne.com.